TRUSTING ABBY

Bayou Nights, Book Three

BARBARA MCMAHON

Trusting Abby
Copyright © 2020 Barbara McMahon
All Rights Reserved

Prologue

Abby Talmadge breezed into the office a woman on a mission. She had it all planned. She just needed to convince her two brothers-in-law. She'd been toying with the idea for more than a week and she had all her ducks in a row. Both were stubborn men, however, and if they said no, she'd go back to square one. But optimism was one of her strong traits and she had to hold on to the belief she'd get her way.

"Good morning," she said, trying to put as much confidence into her manner as possible as she greeted her sister Michelle's new husband. Josh O'Malley was skilled at reading people. It came in handy in his business, that of a private investigator. She didn't want any of her doubts to surface as he'd hone in on them in a heart beat.

She still had trouble believing her sister Michelle had married him on such short acquaintance. But he adored her sister, so for that alone, Abby was happy to welcome him as part of the family.

"Josh," Brandon Madison said in greeting, walking in behind Abby.

Glancing at Brandon, Abby smiled confidently. She'd known him since he'd first married her oldest sister,

Caroline, a bit over six years ago. Totally comfortable around the tech genius, she was counting on him backing her up. He absolutely doted on her sister--especially now that Caroline was pregnant. And after all, Caroline had started this quest to find their father. Now Abby could do something to bring it to a close.

Josh stood and looked warily at the two people who had just invaded his office.

"Good morning, I think. To what do I owe this unexpected honor?"

Brandon shrugged and glanced at Abby. "I'm not sure. This meeting's her idea. And I'm under strict instructions to say nothing about it to Caroline."

"Oh, oh. Sounds like Michelle's last scheme--and I ended up married to her!" Josh said, motioning his visitors to sit. Sinking into his desk chair, he gazed at Abby. "Something tells me I'm not going to like this."

"Ha, shows how much you know." Abby pulled her chair close to the desk and pulled a folder from her tote. Slapping it on the desk, she looked up expectantly.

"Recognize that?"

Josh nodded slowly. "It's the office folder regarding your father's search. Michelle took it a few weeks ago."

"She left it at my place," Abby confirmed. Flicking a glance at Brandon, she turned back to Josh. "You have a dossier for three men who match most of the facts we've compiled on Sam Williams. How long do you think it'll take to visit each of them and interview them? I, for one, am anxious to know if one is my father."

"These things take time, Abby. This is not the only case my firm is working on, you know."

"Well, time's been passing ever since my grandmother trumped up that murder charge that drove our father away before I was even born. How much more time will it take?" Frustration bubbled up.

She'd never known her father. Caroline and Michelle each had a few memories, but she had none. Her mother had died when she was little. She hardly had any memories of her.

All her life, she'd missed the family she should have had due to the evil machinations of her status-proud grandmother. Now that the dream of her life--meeting her father--was close. She was impatient to locate him. The fact Josh had narrowed the field down to a few meant they were so close to identifying her father.

Josh glanced at Brandon and then shrugged. "It's been more than twenty years since he was last seen. When Caroline and Brandon discovered he hadn't left voluntarily a few months ago, Michelle brought what information you had. With the scarcity of information, we've done well to identify these three men as possibles. These things take time."

"You've been on the case since June. It's now the first week in August. How much time do you need? You already have all this information. Why can't we go confront each man and ask if he's our father? We all want to locate him. This delay is intolerable."

"I know. And it'll only take a few more weeks. I need to

travel to each location, arrange to speak privately with each man and go from there. If your father still thinks there's a murder charge hanging over him, I don't want to spook him by phoning first. Progress has been made--we've pretty much narrowed the field down to these three men. Can a few more weeks matter?"

"Maybe not to Caroline or Michelle," Abby said restlessly. "Both obviously have other things on their minds with new husbands, new homes, new families. But I've just finished my last training course at the hospital and have some vacation time coming."

She looked at Brandon and then Josh, smiling triumphantly. "I've thought of a way to speed up this step."

"And that is?" Brandon asked cautiously.

"If we each take one suspect, and make a quick visit to each location, we can have the answer by the end of the week! Brandon often flies to California for business, he could check out the man in Burbank and Caroline would never guess what he's up to, or get her hopes up."

"I think she could handle it," Brandon said dryly. "The doctor says she's healthy as can be. She is not going to miscarry this baby."

"I know. Still, we're all taking great care not to get her stressed or worried. I think if none of these men is our father, she'd be hugely disappointed. Anyway, it doesn't hurt to keep it a secret until we know for sure.

"You, Josh, can go to New Jersey. And I'll go to Houston and check out that one."

"Or we can wait a while longer and I'll visit each in turn and have the answer then," Josh said.

"But I don't want to wait. The timing's perfect right now. I have several weeks vacation due me before I start my new job at the hospital. I'll spend the first couple of days in Houston, talk to the man, and then I'll have plenty of time to enjoy my vacation. You two know how much it means to me and my sisters to find our father."

Brandon leaned back in the visitor's chair and steepled his fingers. "Actually, it's not a bad plan."

"It's a great plan," Abby said with enthusiasm, turning to him in relief, glad Brandon backed her up.

"It could work," Josh added slowly.

Abby beamed at him. "Of course it'll work. Piece of cake. Then it's settled? I'll take the Houston Sam Williams. We can keep in touch by phone. This time next week, we'll know for sure if one of these three is my father!"

Chapter One

Tossing her phone on the bed, Abby paced the small motel room, fuming. She couldn't believe the man! She'd been calm and rational. And he'd accused her of being some kind of fortune-hunting hussy! Ohhh! She clenched her fists, wanting to scream!

Storming over to the window, she slid it open and gazed out over the strip of grass that softened the stark asphalt of the motel. Taking a deep breath, she held it a moment before letting it whoosh out. Reviewing the conversation, she tried to see where it'd gone wrong. What could she have done differently?

She'd asked to speak to Samuel J. Williams, only to be told he was out of the office. Directed to the acting Executive Manager, Dev Hamilton, Abby had been forthright and honest. She'd introduced herself and then explained she was trying to verify if Samuel Williams had lived in Mississippi about twenty-three years ago. If he had been married once to a woman named Talmadge?

Dev Hamilton had not been equally forthcoming. When he'd pressed her as to why she was calling, she had responded she thought she might be Sam Williams' daughter.

The obnoxious man on the other end laughed shortly, then railed at her. How had she discovered Sam was ill? Was that the reason for her obvious ploy of trying to worm her way into some money? Samuel Williams had never lived in Mississippi and if she called again, he'd inform the authorities that she was trying something fraudulent.

Just hearing the echo of his tone ignited her anger. Slapping a hand against the wall beside the window, she whirled around and paced back to the phone. She wished she knew something that could set that arrogant man back on his heels. She wanted nothing from her father but to discover who he was. Where he was living. That he was all right.

Maybe have dinner together to learn what he'd been doing during the last twenty-some years.

Sinking slowly on the bed, she sighed. There was no proof that this man was her father. That was the entire reason for her presence in Houston--to discover if he were. The acting Executive Manager sounded certain the man had never lived in Mississippi. How would he know that?

Maybe Josh or Brandon had already discovered that one of the other men was her father.

She'd phone them to find out before pursuing this further.

But if neither of the other two Samuel Williams proved to be the man they were searching for, then Mr. Hamilton would soon learn that she wasn't easily pushed aside. Discovering the truth was too important to her. She'd find a way!

Snatching up her phone, she punched in the number to Josh's office and waited, frustration still roiling inside.

Six days later Abby slipped the key into a lock and turned it. Opening the door, she peeked inside. With a quick, guilty glance over her shoulder, she lifted her suitcase and entered. The small apartment was hers. The guilt came from the way she'd obtained it.

Closing the door, she set her bag on the floor and went to the window to open the blinds. Sunlight flooded in. Turning, she surveyed the living room.

Neat and austere, it waited only for someone to breathe life into it. The furniture was functional. There were no pictures on the walls. No magazines or books stacked on the coffee table. Nothing to give the room personality. It awaited its next tenant.

Which was her--temporarily.

She stood by the window while she dialed Josh's number. Gazing over the estate while it rang on the other end, Abby grew a tad impatient. Michelle answered.

Taking a deep breath, Abby tried out a fake New York accent. Could it fool anyone who knew her?

"Michelle O'Malley?"

"Yes?"

"I'm trying to reach your husband, Josh."

"I'm sorry, he's unavailable right now. May I take a message?"

"Ask him to call Abby Brown."

"Abby? Is that you?"

"Hi, Michelle. Yes, it's me," Abby said in her normal tone, almost laughing.

"What in the world are you doing? I didn't recognize you at first."

"Good, that was the idea."

"What idea? Where are you? Still in Houston?"

"Yes. Actually, I'm at Sam Williams' home."

"At his house? You got through to him? Is he our father?"

"I have no idea. I've spent the best part of a week trying to get some information about him or trying to arrange an appointment with the acting Executive Manager--who refuses to have anything to do with me or my calls. Samuel Williams is out of the office sick. His secretary is like a bulldog and refuses to tell me anything. Nothing gets by her."

Abby smiled smugly. "Well, almost nothing. I'm trying another way. Circumventing Dev Hamilton and the guardian secretary, if you must know."

"What does that mean? Who's Dev Hamilton?"

"Apparently *the* man in charge in Samuel Williams' absence. Some officer in the company with delusions of omnipotence. He won't even speak to me."

For a moment the frustration surfaced. Taking a deep breath, Abby continued, "One day I went to the offices determined to get in to see somebody who could give me information, but there was a big meeting going on about some oil well crisis and rather than hang around all day, I left. In the elevator on the way out I overheard two secretaries talking about how hard it was proving to find a live-in gardener for the Williams' estate."

"You didn't!" Michelle exclaimed.

"Yep, I faked a résumé, applied and got the job."

"What? Abby, you don't know anything about gardening. You're a nurse."

"How hard can it be to cut back a few flowers? Anyway, I only need to pretend for a day or two. It's the only way I could get anywhere close. When I originally tried to explain the situation to Mr. Hamilton on the phone, he immediately tagged me as a gold-digger and threatened to call the authorities."

Michelle murmured, "Why?"

"I reviewed the biography Josh put together for this Sam Williams. He's loaded, so I can see why Hamilton might think someone showing up out of the blue when Sam Williams was sick was looking to cash in. Once I can get in to see Sam Williams, talk to him face-to-face, I'll have the answer and be on my way. But just in case they check references before I can get in to see him, I listed you. And I said I was Abby Brown. And that I'm from New York. I can't take the chance Mr. Hamilton will recognize my voice if he's running interference here as well as at the office. So if they call to check, say I was the best gardener you ever had."

"I can't believe you. This is the craziest stunt I've heard. And why Abby Brown?"

"I had to come up with something since I'd told the secretary that first day that I was Abby Talmadge."

"You'll never get away with this. I can't believe you are already hired. They must really be hard up for gardeners in Houston."

"It seemed like a good idea at the time. And it's for a live in gardener. Though I can't imagine why."

Abby waved her hand in the air as if brushing away a minor detail. "Anyway, if anyone calls, make sure to back me up on this. Have you heard anything more from Josh or Brandon?"

"I don't expect Josh to call until later, but he did finally get an appointment with the man in New Jersey. Brandon's guy is still out of town and won't be back until next week. Brandon's not staying away from Caroline that long, so he'll have to make another trip to the West Coast."

Abby shook her head. "Last week I thought for sure we'd know by now, and yet here we are with none of the suspects eliminated."

Michelle laughed softly. "Suspects, indeed. You make them sound like criminals. One could be our father."

"Well, I don't know what else to call them. I'm not unpacking until I see if I can catch this Sam Williams today. I don't know how ill he is, but unless he's bedridden, maybe I can run into him right away. Don't you think he's sure to walk around the yard at some point? Fresh air and sunshine is always good for convalescing individuals."

"Unpacking?"

"I get an apartment over the garage included as part of the package for the job."

"Good grief. How in the world did you get hired?"

Michelle asked. Abby could hear the incredulity in her sister's voice and smiled again.

"Well, I fudged a bit on the qualifications," Abby said, delighting in the way things had turned out.

Her attention was drawn to the snazzy black sports car that pulled to a stop in front of the garage--powerful, with sleek lines. A rich man's toy. The driver climbed out and looked around. He was tall, dark and gorgeous.

"Wow," she said softly.

"What?"

"You should see what just drove up. Oh my gosh, he's heading for the steps that lead up here. I've got to go."

Pressing off, Abby pulled her suitcase into the bedroom. Two seconds later she heard the rap on the door.

Running her fingers through her short blond hair, she took a deep breath. Checking to make sure her linen slacks and light-weight top were still tidy, she reached for the doorknob. If this was the owner of the estate, he definitely wasn't her missing father--too young by far.

She opened the door and almost stopped breathing. Tall, dark and gorgeous, all right--even half hidden behind the mirrored lenses of his sunglasses. He wore a dress shirt, opened at the throat, sleeves rolled partway up; his tie loosened, and dark charcoal-gray slacks. The clothes couldn't camouflage the rugged width of his shoulders, nor his height--which had to be over six feet.

The dark glasses hid his expression. What color were his eyes? Dark and yummy like the rest of him, she bet, wishing he'd take them off.

"Abby Brown?" he asked.

Her attention was instantly caught and her heart dropped. His voice was the one she'd heard over the phone when she'd first called the oil company's headquarters. Deep and husky, reminding her of sultry nights in the bayou. This was Dev Hamilton. What was he doing here?

She took a shaky breath, her heart racing. Would he recognize her voice despite her fake accent? Kick her out before she had a chance to locate and talk with Sam Williams? Call the authorities?

She nodded. Pure dumb luck got her here--but some fast thinking would be needed to stay!

"Yes."

"Dev Hamilton," he said, holding out his hand. "Sorry I didn't get a chance to meet you at the office. My secretary, Janice, told me she'd hired you."

Abby boldly placed her hand in his, almost snatching it back when an unexpected jolt of electricity shot up her arm. Eyes wide, she stared at him, her heart thundering in her chest. What did he want? Why was he here?

"I thought I was hired to work for a Samuel Williams," she said, trying the New York accent again. If she could fool Michelle for a few seconds, surely she could fool a man who had only spoken with her once briefly on the phone.

"That's right. Samuel's my stepfather." Dev turned around and looked over the neglected grounds. "This is my folks' home. They've been away for a few weeks, the gardener gone even longer as I'm sure you can tell by the state of the yard."

Samuel was Dev's stepfather?

Oh, no! That meant Dev would probably be checking up on her all the time. That was the last thing she needed.

Trying to keep the dismay off her face, Abby peeked over his shoulder. The garden looked fine to her. Maybe the grass was a bit overgrown. And some of the flowers had passed their prime and obviously needed to be trimmed. A tiny bit of doubt crept in. She knew nothing about gardening. Weeds, crabgrass and fertilizers were abstract concepts to her. She'd never followed the gardener around Talmadge Hall when she was a kid. And she'd lived in apartments since leaving there.

Hope was beginning to dim that she could confront Samuel Williams, confirm whether he was her father, and depart before anyone discovered how inept she was.

Suddenly she realized what he'd said. If Samuel Williams was out of town, she couldn't see him today. The secretary had told her the man was away but Abby had thought she meant away from the *office*, sick at home. How ill could he be if he could travel?

"I noticed," she said in the growing silence. Thoughts tumbled in her mind. When would the man return?

When Dev turned to face her, she took an involuntary step backward.

"I expect them home next weekend."

Next weekend? Today was Wednesday; that made their return nine days away. Abby hoped her surprised dismay didn't show in her expression. She had no idea if she could fake being a gardener for nine whole days!

"Can you have the place in shape by then? I could have hired a landscape service, but my mother likes to have one person take care of everything. And be on hand daily to advise her when she has questions," he continued.

"Sure," she said, careful to keep all hints of her usual Southern drawl from her voice.

She dare not mention she hadn't a clue what gardening entailed. Her grandmother had a couple of men to care for the grounds at Talmadge Hall, where Abby had grown up, but she had always preferred playing on the banks of the Mississippi River when a child to tagging after the yard workers.

"I assume my secretary reviewed everything with you."

Nodding, she tried to remember what they'd discussed. The impersonation had been a spur-of-the-moment attempt. She'd been so surprised the woman hired her, she hadn't paid much attention to details. Why should she, she thought she'd be gone by nightfall.

But not if Sam Williams was away from home.

Could she stay more than a week without anyone discovering the truth?

Highly unlikely.

She was so close, darn it!

Maybe Josh or Brandon would have better luck. Maybe she didn't need to talk to this man at all if either of the others proved to be her father.

Dev looked at her suspiciously. "How old are you?"

Flustered, Abby forgot her future worry for an immediate one. How much experience would a gardener have? She'd indicated several years on her fake résumé, which meant she had to be--how old?

"How old do I look?" she asked, stalling. The dark glasses disconcerted her. She could tell a lot by watching the expressions in a person's eyes.

"Twenty."

She smiled and shook her head, hoping he couldn't tell how her heart raced. "The benefit of great genes--I'm twenty-six." Well, adding four years to her real age wasn't too unbelievable, was it?

His patent look of disbelief shook her. What if he called her bluff, asked to see a driver's license or other proof of age? Or even proof she was who she said she was?

"Been gardening all your life?" he asked in mock disbelief.

Abby nodded, trying not to fidget. Trying to remember the details of that fake résumé. If he started to cross-examine her, she'd really feel like an idiot. But it didn't matter. If it came to that, she could always leave--and never have to see this disturbing individual again. Josh could handle it.

But that also meant she couldn't contact Sam Williams. This entire scheme was her idea. She had to follow it through. She dare not do less than her best after convincing Josh and Brandon to go along with the idea.

Dev slid his hands into his pockets and pulled out a small bunch of keys on a circular key ring, holding them out to her.

Abby automatically held out her hand.

"For the shed, the mower and the garage. My secretary obviously gave you the keys for the apartment," he said.

Abby nodded.

"Any questions?"

She shook her head, feeling as tongue-tied as a schoolgirl. Now if he would just get in that sexy car and head out, she could decide how to pretend to be a gardener for nine days.

"Come on, then. I'll show you around." Dev stood back on the small landing, waiting for her.

Abby stepped out, too close to the man. She could feel waves of heat and energy emanating from him. Taking a breath, she drew in the tangy scent of his aftershave. And something else. Some distinctive essence that was Dev Hamilton's own. Suddenly every cell in her body seemed attuned to him.

Her reaction floored her. She almost stumbled as she hurried down the steps, astonished by the wave of pure sensual awareness that swept through her. Good grief, this man would have a hissy fit if he even suspected who she was. And she didn't want to guess what he'd do if he discovered her deception. If he threatened to call the authorities over a phone call, what would happen if he found out she had lied her way onto his stepfather's estate?

Maybe *her* father's estate as well, she reminded herself.

"This way," he said, touching her shoulder lightly.

That confusing tingling darted across her skin at his touch. Sidestepping, Abby tried to maintain a calm expression. She must not let him guess a mere whisper of contact affected her in any way.

She felt as awkward as a first-semester nursing student

flustered by some doctor. She'd survived that, so she could survive a few minutes with Dev Hamilton--as long as he didn't touch her again.

They walked around the side of the garage, along by the fence, across the grassy lawn.

"What do you think so far?" Dev asked.

Clearing her throat, she shrugged and tried to look like she was assessing the state of the grounds. Feeling she needed to say something, Abby nodded toward a bank of roses, some already past their prime. "Nice roses."

"My mother's pride and joy. And Dad indulges her. She must have more than fifty varieties. They take a lot of care, as I'm sure you know."

"Right." Had she heard that somewhere before?

Taking a breath, she decided to skip any attempt at conversation. If the only thing they had in common was flowers, she'd give herself away in an instant even if he didn't recognize her voice. She was lucky she'd identified the roses!

"This is the gardener's shed," Dev said, as they rounded a high hedge and stopped before a small wooden structure.

He waited a moment. "You have the keys."

Abby frowned, embarrassed to be reminded. She stepped to the door and located the correct key to open the knob. Dev stood only a few feet away watching her every move. She wished she didn't feel so conscious of the man. She was used to working around dynamic men all the time. Didn't she spend her days with interns and surgeons and visiting doctors?

Opening the door, she threw it wide, gazing in

bewilderment at the assortment of tools and gardening implements. The shed was immaculate.

Dev watched her, so Abby stepped inside, a bright smile spreading. She hoped it didn't look as false as it felt.

"Great, everything I need."

It was dark in the shed and when Dev stepped in, he withdrew his dark glasses. Abby caught his gaze on her.

At least the question of his eye color was settled--silvery gray. He stared at her until she realized how many seconds were ticking by.

It was almost a physical effort to drag her gaze away to look at the huge rider-mower. Her heart raced, her palms felt damp and she had to resist the urge to look back over her shoulder at him.

She could maintain this aloof, disinterested pose until he left. Then she'd collapse on the sofa in the apartment and search for some perspective. She was not cut out for this kind of subterfuge. Undercover investigative work was not proving to be easy. How did her brother-in-law ever manage?

"The household staff will return on Saturday. My folks will be home the following Saturday. Does that give you enough time to get the grounds in shape?"

"Sure."

Enough time to totally mess up everything if she wasn't careful. Blast it, why hadn't the secretary mentioned Samuel Williams wasn't actually in residence? Abby never would have concocted such a wild scheme if she hadn't thought she could somehow get in to see the man today and get some answers immediately.

Dev glanced around. "I'll leave you to it then. If you need anything, give me a call." He handed her a business card.

Abby was a fast learner. She took the card, being careful not to let her fingers touch his. Nerves probably accounted for the wild tingling sensations, but she was not taking any more chances.

"Thanks."

She stood in the dim shed and watched him walk away. Slowly she let out her breath. Time to make some decisions. Stay or give up and return home. Maybe Josh was right, she should have let him continue the investigation at his own pace.

Except she wanted to know now not when his business let him focus on this case.

Dev headed for his car, a niggling sense of something wrong tugging at his mind. Did it have to do with Abby Brown? She struck him as nervous. And young. Definitely young. As soon as he reached the office in the morning he'd talk with Janice and review Abby's résumé. He knew Janice would have been thorough in the interview process yet something bothered him about his mother's new gardener.

Maybe it was the fact she was so pretty. Her short blond hair looked like sunshine. Her eyes were as blue as the Gulf on a summer's day. Slim and trim, she certainly looked capable of doing the work, but there was something that just didn't mesh.

He paused by his car and glanced up at the apartment. If his mother hadn't been so insistent about hiring a new gardener after Luis had retired, he'd have contracted for a service to come in weekly. Now they had a stranger living over the garage.

Not that it mattered, but he suddenly remembered the call last week from a woman purporting to be his stepfather's long-lost daughter. They had done their best to keep the extent of his dad's illness from the media. No sense making waves in the oil industry with word about how ill Samuel had been--a delayed diagnosis of acute appendicitis and the resulting toxicity because of it, which the doctors had thankfully caught in time. He was recovering and would live another forty years with luck. And be back to work within the month.

But Dev's mother was taking no chances--she'd insisted Samuel make a complete recovery before even thinking about returning. Hence their cruise.

Even so, the business sharks could smell blood. Dev had better warn Abby to say nothing about his parents to anyone.

Heading back for the shed he rounded the corner and bumped right into her. Reaching out to steady her, he caught her arms. The soft skin beneath her short sleeves was warm and silky. Her eyes widened in surprise as she looked up into his face. For one odd moment, Dev wanted to pull her closer, wrap his arms around her and feel her warm lips beneath his.

"Oops," she said, pulling back. "I thought you left."

"I forgot something." Slowly he dropped his hands,

closing them as if he could capture the soft texture of her skin and imprint it on his fingertips.

"I already locked the shed."

"It's not that. No one is to know my folks aren't home. And when they get back, no one gets in to see them unless the housekeeper admits them."

"Why?"

"Samuel Williams is big news in these parts. I had a crackpot trying to pass herself off as Dad's daughter a few days ago. Probably heard he was ill and thought to cash in on the estate if he died. It occurs to me that she or someone like her might find out where he lives and try another way. Just be alert and don't let in strangers."

"Since everyone will be a stranger to me, I guess I wouldn't let anyone in," she said slowly. Crackpot, huh?

"There's no danger. Just be alert. Dad's still recovering and I don't want him worried with anything--especially some stranger trying a shakedown or the press trying for some exclusive."

"Fine, no strangers trying a shakedown, no paparazzi." She nodded.

Dev hesitated, wondering about the glint in her eyes. There was nothing more to say. Yet he was reluctant to leave.

That jolt of awareness when he'd held her seemed to awaken his curiosity. He wanted to learn more about Abby Brown. Where she was from? Why she had selected gardening as a profession?

Was there a man in her life?

"All set?" he asked, squashing the last thought. He didn't need any complications of that sort. And the last woman he'd get involved with was some charming gardener--he'd learned his lesson. If and when he was ready to start a family, he'd pick someone from his own social strata--to make sure she wasn't marrying him for his money!

She nodded again.

Fascinated despite his need to return to the office, he hesitated another moment, studying her. He noticed the faint pink color invading her cheeks--which served to make the blue of her eyes even more brilliant. He wanted to touch her again to see if her skin was as hot or if the wash of pink was cool to the touch.

Annoyed at his sudden interest, he spun around. "I'll be here tomorrow afternoon. If you need anything before then, call the office," he said.

He had to get back to work. There were still reports to read, letters to answer and that situation in the Middle East to monitor.

This time when he reached his car, he slid behind the wheel. Just before he pulled away he glanced up and saw her in the rear view mirror. She paused at the bottom of the steps to the garage apartment and stared after him.

Gunning the sports car, he took off. The next time he saw her, maybe he'd get his newest employee to say something more than a few short sentences. He found he was curious about her as he hadn't been about a woman in a long time.

Abby waited until the sleek black car was lost from view

before dashing up the stairs to her new apartment. Closing the door behind her, she leaned against it.

Phew! The man was deadly. When she'd walked into him a few moments ago, she'd thought her heart would stop. His chest had been rock-hard and his reflexes lightning-swift to catch her like that.

His hands on her arms had ignited sensations she'd never experienced. For one crazy moment she'd wished he'd pulled her close and kissed her. She'd never felt so aware of an adult male before. Or so aware of herself as a woman.

She worked with men all the time, dated more than her share, had two sexy brothers-in-law. But they all paled in comparison after a few moments with Dev Hamilton.

Her heart rate gradually slowed.

At least he hadn't connected her with that phone call.

Frowning, she pushed away from the door. His comment rankled. She was *not* some crackpot trying to cash in on her father's wealth.

She reached for her phone and quickly called Michelle.

"Hi, Josh just called. He wants you to call him," Michelle said when she answered.

"Good, I need to talk to him. Was the New Jersey man the one we're looking for?"

"Nope."

"I guess that would have made it too easy."

It certainly would have let her off the hook.

"I know, I wish he'd been the one, but Josh was definite. Are you still at the Williams' place?"

"Yes. Give me Josh's phone number and I'll call him."

"Then call me back and let me know what's going on."

"Will do."

"Wait a minute, Penny wants to say hello."

Two seconds later Abby heard Michelle's step-daughter's voice. She chatted for a few minutes with the four-year-old, remembering how quickly the little girl had taken to her at Michelle and Josh's wedding. She already missed her. While her sister had only been married since the end of June, Abby felt as if she'd known Penny for ages. She planned to spend some of her vacation with her, maybe taking her to the park and the zoo.

That is, if she managed to get home before her vacation was over.

If Sam Williams didn't return until next weekend, did that mean she was stuck here until then? Was there some faster way to discover if he was her father?

As soon as she got Josh's number, she phoned.

"So the New Jersey man isn't the right one," she said when he answered.

"No. And Brandon can't get in touch with the man in California until next week."

"Well, he's not the only one. This one's away from home until next weekend. That's nine days away. There was nothing in the file about a stepson, but I met a man today who claims that distinction."

"Umm," Josh said slowly. "Wait a minute."

Abby heard the rustle of papers in the background.

"Here it is. Samuel Williams married a Ruth Hamilton ten years ago." More papers rustled. "And Ruth had a seventeen-year-old son, Deveraugh Hamilton. This is her second marriage."

"Why wasn't that in the file Michelle left at my place?" Abby wished she'd had some warning.

Though would knowing about him have prepared her for her reaction to the man?

"We were behind in the paperwork at the office because of staffing problems. I'm caught up now, but this information wasn't typed and in the file when she took it."

"I wonder if raising a son compensated for losing his daughters," she mused. "So he's still a contender."

"Not that he had much time to raise the step-son. The kid went to college a couple of years after his mother married Sam. That said, your guy's moved up to a fifty-fifty shot. Where are you?" Josh said.

Abby told him, wishing she could find the humor in the situation when Josh laughed. He didn't have to deal with Dev Hamilton.

"Now what do I do?" she asked.

"Bluff your way through and hope no one looks too deeply into your background. Once the house is opened, see if you can get inside and find anything that might confirm he's the one we're looking for."

"I can't break into the man's house!" Abby was horrified.

"I'm not saying break in. Once the household staff's in place, you can deliver flowers to the various rooms. Arrange them before you take them in and get the help to let you put them where you think they'll look the best. If you start soon enough, you'll become a part of the background, so to speak, and by the end of next week they won't even notice you wandering around. Find a study or home office or check out the bedroom--the usual places people keep important things."

"Josh, I'm not a spy, I don't know the usual places."

"Where would *you* hide something?"

"Oh, just look there, huh?"

"It's a start. Keep in touch."

Abby made sure he had her phone number before she hung up. If Brandon found out the California Sam Williams was her father, she'd be out of here in a heartbeat!

In the meantime, it looked like she was the Williams' new gardener--at least for the next week and a half. She just hoped they arrived home before she annihilated the plants and killed the grass. Somehow working in a hospital emergency room seemed far simpler in comparison.

Chapter Two

By late the next afternoon, Abby was hot and cranky and bone tired. She'd spent hours on YouTube trying to get a handle on all the different aspects of yard maintenance. Thanks to the on-line tutorial, she figured out how to operate the rider-mower and managed to cut the grass. Until she had gotten the knack of driving the thing, however, she'd gone off track a couple of times into the beds near the back wall--and mown some of the flowers right down to the dirt.

She hoped she could find a nursery nearby to buy replacement plants to fill in the now bare spots.

But not yet. She threw herself down on the apron of the pristine swimming pool she'd discovered in her exploration of the estate. Tastefully surrounded by shrubbery and a wide patio, it was a gem. Kicking off her shoes, she scooted to the edge and dangled her feet in the cool water. It felt heavenly. Sighing, she wished she'd brought a bathing suit. But except for the jeans she'd packed for casual wear, the suit she'd brought to wear when meeting Sam, and a couple of blouses, she had a very limited wardrobe.

How naive she'd been to think she could fly in one day, confront a man who, if he were her father had been successfully evading her family for more than twenty years, and be back in New Orleans within a day.

Since it looked as if she was stuck in Houston for another week, it was time to make a quick stop somewhere for clothes. And first thing she'd buy would be a bathing suit. If no one was home, how could anyone object to her using the pool?

She could imagine her grandmother throwing a fit if any of the hired help had even suggested using one of the owner's amenities at Talmadge Hall. Not that they'd had a pool, but the idea was the same.

"But what they don't know can't hurt them," she said, leaning back on her hands, wishing she could slip into the water and revitalize tired muscles by swimming or just plain floating on the surface.

"Making yourself at home?" a familiar, disturbing voice asked behind her.

Abby scrambled to her feet and turned. Dev Hamilton stood only three feet away. Had he heard her talking to herself? Good grief, she'd forgotten to use her fake accent.

He'd foregone the dark glasses today, though the afternoon sun was still high enough to warrant their use. His expression was impassive, his eyes sharp.

She wondered what he was thinking.

"Sorry."

New York twang firmly in place, she reached for her shoes, clutching them to her chest like a shield. "No one was home, I didn't think it'd be a problem just to see how the water felt."

She tried to sidle around him, but he put out a hand to stop her gripping her arm gently.

For a moment Abby's mind went blank. She couldn't step away. She could only stare at Dev, feel the warmth of his palm, and wonder if he felt her heart race.

He looked tired. And formidable. Had he discovered her ruse? Had he seen the decimated flower beds and come to exact retribution?

"It isn't a problem," he said, releasing her.

"What?"

Maybe she was more tired than she suspected. What was he talking about?

He shrugged and tossed a pile of mail on one of the small tables. "There won't be a problem if you use the pool when my folks aren't home. And it's hot today. Go for a swim if you like."

Abby looked longingly at the cool water. "Thanks. But I don't have a bathing suit with me."

He frowned. "Why not?"

"I, um, didn't know I'd be starting so soon. Or that there'd be a pool. I only have an overnight bag with me."

"Are you having your clothes sent?"

"Uh, yes. Soon."

He indicated one of the lounge chairs. "Have a seat."

Warily she sat on the edge, still holding her shoes. Lowering them to her lap she watched him warily. What did he want now? Any kind of conversation with the man was dangerous. She was walking a tightrope as it was and couldn't afford to give anything away.

"According to your résumé and your interview with Janice, you're from New York. But recently you were working for a family in New Orleans, the O'Malleys. Why did you move here?" he asked as he placed a foot on the end of the chaise, leaning over slightly.

Abby tried to come up with a quick answer, but she was too aware of him. He was too close. She could see the fine lines that radiated around his eyes. Feel the heat from his body, her own temperature climbing. Smell the lingering trace of his aftershave.

Her insides quivered like jelly.

What was the question?

"Move here?" she asked, stalling. The secretary hadn't asked her that.

Dev said nothing, just watched her, his eyes narrowing slightly.

"My sister's about to have a baby. I want to be close to her. See the baby grow up," Abby improvised rapidly, sticking as close to the truth as she could. And it was all true, except Caroline did not live in Houston.

He nodded.

She relaxed a bit. Maybe she could get through this. Unless--a horrible thought occurred to her.

"You don't live here, do you?" she asked, hoping her trepidation didn't show.

"Not normally. But I'm house-sitting while my folks are gone."

He straightened and walked over to the table to pick up the stack of envelopes and catalogs. Glancing at her, he paused.

"Do you have a problem with that?"

"No, of course not."

"You get settled in okay?"

Abby nodded. "I found a grocery store last night, so I'm all set. I got started first thing this morning," she said virtuously.

"I saw the grass had been cut. It makes a big difference already."

He tapped the mail against one hand, lost in thought.

Abby stood, ready to take flight as soon as she thought she could do so without arousing his suspicions. Warily watching him, she again noticed how tired he looked. Working too hard, she bet.

Without thinking, she said, "I'm fixing supper soon. Would you like to share it with me? If you don't have other plans. Then you could tell me more about the estate and what your mother likes in the way of flowers. I think fresh flowers in a home add a lot to a welcoming feeling."

Good grief, had those words come from her mouth?

Danger, danger, danger.

The mere thought of spending more time with him put her on alert. How odd would he find a newly hired employee inviting the boss to dinner?

Yet what could be a better way to casually ask questions about Samuel Williams? Maybe she'd find out something that would definitely eliminate him.

"It's nothing fancy," she added as he hesitated. She'd have to be careful, but most people liked to talk about their families and if she could glean some information it'd be worth the risk.

"Okay, you're on. I'll take a quick shower and change."

Walking back to her small apartment a couple of minutes later, she wondered how she could draw him out without causing any suspicion. If she succeeded, maybe she could consider a new career working as a private investigator for Josh--if she ever got tired of nursing.

Dev showered and donned a comfortable pair of old shorts and a clean short-sleeve shirt. Work took its toll, especially doing twice the normal load in covering for his father.

Tonight offered a change of pace--eating dinner with the new gardener.

She was nothing like the women he usually dated. Not that this was a date--just a friendly invitation for a meal. It had surprised him, but maybe she was lonely. Though he couldn't see that if her sister lived in Houston. Why wasn't she spending time with her?

Or was her invitation an attempt to kiss up to the boss?

He laughed and reached for the phone. Not likely. Her wide blue eyes seemed guileless and honest. She hadn't tried to flirt. It was probably that she wanted to learn more about the people she'd be working for.

He'd be glad to have a quiet meal. Lately squiring women around expensive restaurants and nightclubs downtown had paled. He still attended events that would help generate more business or keep current customers happy. But they no longer held the same appeal or excitement as they once had.

He dialed the garage apartment.

"Hello?"

"Abby?" Did the sound of her voice jog a memory?

"Yes."

He was imagining things. That New York accent was particularly her own.

"Dev here. I thought we could eat by the pool, if you like."

"Why sure, if that's allowed. I made a chef's salad and heated some rolls. I think there'll be enough to fill you up. I'll bring it over."

"I'll be there in a minute to help you carry the things out."

"Okay."

Satisfied there would be no romantic overtones to the meal, Dev headed for the garage.

Entering her apartment a few minutes later, he looked around. He didn't see any appreciable difference to the room except for the small bouquet of roses on the coffee table-- the blossoms past their prime. He remembered her comment about flowers in a home.

"Nice flowers," he commented.

She flushed and nodded. "They're a bit past their peak, but I didn't want to just let them wither on the branch. And they still smell fragrant."

Just like a gardener, he thought, couldn't let go of flowers.

"Take some fresh ones next time," he said. "My mother loves to have fresh flowers in the house."

"Great, I'll be sure and have some at the house when she

returns. I'll do arrangements for every room downstairs. Maybe the housekeeper can give me a tour when she gets back."

"Or I can later."

She nodded, and then gestured to a small tray laden with plates and glasses.

"The salad's ready and the rolls will be done in another minute or two. Want to carry out the plates and iced tea?"

Settled on the deck around the pool a few minutes later, shaded from the sinking sun by one of the huge umbrellas his mother insisted on, Dev began to relax. It was quiet and peaceful. Abby sat across the small table. She hadn't made eye contact once. In fact, he wondered if she felt ill at ease. She wore her jeans, but had obviously taken time to shower. Her hair was still a bit damp and her shirt fresh and clean.

And hugging her figure. Her very feminine, delectable figure. Outdoor work must be good for keeping muscles toned and weight off. She looked fit and sexy.

"Aren't you hungry?" he asked as she took another sip of tea. He needed something to take his mind off that line of thought. He had no business thinking about her figure!

"Actually, I nibbled a bit while preparing the salad," she confessed. "I was starved then. Is this enough for you? I expect being from Texas, you'd much rather eat beef."

"And being from New York, you'd probably prefer a Coney Island hot dog."

She smiled and shook her head. "I like salads. Will all this fill you up?"

"With the rolls." He looked at her. "Thanks for dinner."

"So tell me all about your family," she invited a minute or two later as the silence stretched out.

"What exactly do you want to know?"

"What it was like growing up here? Did you play football? Did your father coach Little League? Did he teach you to swim? Whatever."

"I didn't grow up here. My mom married Sam when I was in high school. They bought this place during my last year. Before that my mother and I lived closer to Galveston. Yes, I played some ball in high school, but didn't in college. I like to swim, but I learned to do that long before my mother married Sam. The pool's Dad's pride and joy, however."

Dev launched into a tale about how his dad convinced his mother to agree to a pool when they were still negotiating on the house. And then how he and Samuel had *helped* the contractor--causing more problems than they solved. Dev had a way of making his stepfather sound like a perfect parent, caring, and yet able to let Dev make some mistakes to learn life lessons.

Laughing at one of his comments, he liked the way she laughed. Wishing to get to know the new gardener a bit more, he said, "Tell me more about yourself. Were you born and raised in New York?"

She hesitated. For a moment, he wondered if there was something about New York she didn't want to talk about.

"I always think of New York as concrete canyons and Times Square," he said wondering about her hesitation.

"There're plenty of neighborhoods with gardens and yards. And Central Park takes up a lot of real estate," she said.

"Are you and your sister the only ones?"

"I have two sisters," Abby said slowly.

Dev took his roll and broke off a piece, buttering it. "Are both living here in Houston?"

She shook her head.

When she didn't follow up on that answer, he asked, "What do your parents do?"

"I never knew them. My mother died right after I was born and my father had gone before her."

"That's tough. I'm sorry."

She nodded.

"My mother divorced my real father when I was just a little kid. We never saw him again. She married Sam when I was sixteen. I think of him as my father. He and I are closer than my mother and I."

Dev popped the roll into his mouth, wondering why he'd told Abby that bit of information. It was not something he normally talked about to strangers--or even friends for that matter.

"Then lucky you. Our grandmother raised us."

"I have been lucky. You'll like him when you meet him. He's fair and honest. Works hard. Plays hard, too. And he's crazy about my mother. Which helps make up for her first marriage which wasn't that happy."

"Is this your Dad's first marriage?" she asked casually, tracing a pattern on the condensation of her glass.

Dev looked at her sharply. "Yes," he said.

"Tell me about your family vacations. Where was the best spot your parents took you?" she said, quickly changing the subject.

For the next few minutes, Dev regaled her with outlandish stories of his teen years, embellished from time to time to impress such an avid listener. He spoke often of his parents, always with fondness.

Growing silent, he looked over at her. The sun was sinking behind the trees. Twilight would descend soon. The evening had sped by.

She looked up then and met his gaze. Her eyes were mischievous. Leaning forward slightly, she smiled. "If you go inside now, I could come back here later and go skinny-dipping. That pool still looks mighty inviting."

Dev smiled. Gotcha, he thought. She was just like the others, a little slower in making her move, that was all.

"What if I stay?" he suggested provocatively.

Her smile faded. Her manner became distant. "Then I'll have to wait until I get a bathing suit. I'll take a cool shower to relax instead. Are you finished?"

"Yes."

"Then, good night." She stood and began stacking the dishes.

"I'll help take the things in with you."

She looked at him. Shaking her head slowly, she picked up the tray with their stacked dishes. "I can manage. Thanks for sharing dinner with me. I get lonely sometimes at mealtimes. The rest of the time, I'm fine. But eating alone isn't all that much fun."

He watched her walk toward the garage apartment, her head held high, balancing the heavy tray as if it were light as a feather.

So much for thinking Abby Brown was like everyone else he'd ever met. He'd thought her comment about skinny-dipping was her way of suggesting their relationship take another direction. He'd misread the signs.

She intrigued him, no denying that. Stretching out on the lounge chair, he relaxed. He was tired. Trying to keep up with his own work and his father's, juggling the myriad of unfamiliar tasks while doing his own workload was challenging but also draining. Tonight was a rare evening since his father left the hospital that he hadn't stayed at the office until long after dark.

Though maybe dinner could have been considered working late--interviewing a new employee. Except now that he thought about their conversation, he'd done more of the talking. He still didn't feel he knew Abby Brown. What made her tick? Why had she left the place where she'd been born and raised to move first to New Orleans, then follow a sister to Houston?

He hadn't learned anything about her sisters.

But he'd learned Abby listened like she hung on every word he uttered. That her wide blue eyes could look at a man like he was special, without flirting or teasing.

And her laugh enchanted him.

Frowning, Dev studied the pool. He was *not* enchanted. He was mildly interested in the new gardener--nothing more!

Maybe tomorrow he'd leave work early enough to invite her out to dinner in return for tonight's meal. And see what else he could discover.

Abby quickly cleaned up. Turning off the light in the tiny

kitchen, she gazed out over the yard. Lights now illuminated the pool area and some of the flower beds visible from her window. But she couldn't see Dev. Was he still sitting by the water or had he gone inside?

Tempted to sneak near the pool to check it out, she firmly squelched the idea. She wanted a swim, but not enough to risk running into him again tonight. If she only knew if his stepfather was her real father, things could be so different. She'd have some idea about how to handle things.

But right now, everything was too uncertain. And she couldn't afford to be discovered. Not until she had a chance to meet Sam Williams.

Dev's tales of his teenage years haunted her. He spoke with such love and affection about both his mother and Sam. Her only childhood memories were of her grandmother's rather stern ideas of raising girls to be ladies. There'd been no family camping vacations, no trips to the beach or Disney World.

Not that it mattered now. She had a good job and could afford to go wherever she wanted for vacation.

"Yeah, right. So how come you're in Houston working as a gardener?" she asked as she wandered into the bedroom. Taking off her jeans, she lay down on the bed, trying to relax her muscles. She was used to hard work-turning patients, carrying heavy trays of medicines, making beds, on her feet all day. But today she'd used some different muscles and now paid the price.

Maybe later she'd see if the pool was deserted, but right now she was too tired to even move.

It was after midnight when Abby awoke. She moved restlessly on the bed, her back and shoulders aching.

Sitting up, she pulled on her jeans and caught a towel from the bathroom. Walking across the dark yard to the pool she checked out the house to make sure no lights were on. Dev was sound asleep by now. The outdoor lights had to be on a timer. They were no longer illuminating the pool or gardens.

Slipping off her jeans and shirt at the edge of the pool, she slipped into the inviting water, wearing only a bra and panties.

The coolness felt great against her heated skin. Slowly, making as little noise as possible she swam for a while, then flipped over and floated. The stars were brilliant against the dark velvet of the night sky, the moon was just a sliver in the western horizon. August nights in Houston were just as hot and humid as in New Orleans. Abby enjoyed the refreshing cool water against her skin.

It was late by the time she reluctantly climbed from the pool. Dripping, she wrung water from her hair. It wouldn't take long for the sultry heat to evaporate the water from her skin and hair. Feeling refreshed, relaxed and ready for sleep, she picked up her jeans and shirt and wandered back to her apartment enjoying the quiet night.

Would she be able to take advantage of the pool when the rest of the household returned?

If not officially, she could always sneak in after everyone was asleep.

Bright and early the next morning Abby planned her day.

First thing she needed to do was to find a clothing store, then a nursery. She counted on the nursery people to give her hints beyond what she'd learned on YouTube. She needed enough information to pass muster to any casual questions. Her primary goal, however, was to stay away from people who would ask them.

She didn't trust the intelligence she'd seen in Dev's eye. He was astute. If she slipped, he'd pounce on any mistake instantly.

And send her packing.

Which she didn't want at least for another eight days. One day closer to meeting Sam Williams of Houston. That was the primary objective.

Staying had nothing to do with wishing to see Dev again. Though if he came home early tonight, maybe she'd just happen to be in the yard. And if she thought of ordering a large pizza on the spur of the moment, could he fault her for that?

Opening the door a few minutes later, she stopped at the sight of the neatly folded towel she'd forgotten by the pool. A note rested on top.

It's dangerous to swim alone. Next time wake me!

Slipping the note into her pocket, Abby almost laughed. As if it wouldn't be twice as dangerous to go swimming after midnight with a man like Dev Hamilton and in her underwear of all things!

Abby's thoughts returned to Dev again and again as she went through the day. What if they met under different circumstances? Would he even look at a nurse? From the few things he'd mentioned last evening, she knew he was used to dating more sophisticated women--the kind her grandmother had tried so hard to mold Abby into.

Not that it mattered. Once she left Houston, she'd never see Dev again.

It was odd how the thought brought feelings of disappointment and regret.

By seven that evening, Abby gave up. He wasn't coming by the house as she had hoped. There was only so much she could pretend to be doing and not get dirty. She'd cleaned up at four, donned one of the new shorts and sleeveless tops she'd bought that morning. Just a hint of makeup to enhance her eyes and she'd been set.

Carefully cutting dead blossoms, she began working near the garage. It was Friday night. He probably had a date. But just in case, she wanted to be in the vicinity if he arrived home.

Gradually moving along the fence, she now worked behind the house and still no sign of Dev's fancy sports car. She might as well call for that pizza and find another way to spend her evening. He wasn't showing up after all.

"Which is just as well," she mumbled as she put away the clippers and dumped the dead flowers in the compost pile she'd found behind the shed. "You have no business getting involved at all with Samuel Williams' stepson. Identify the man and take it from there.

If he's your father, what next?"

She stopped dead, suddenly realizing she hadn't a clue what she and her sisters would do once they located the man. Vaguely there had been talk about making sure he wasn't in want.

If this man was their father, he was definitely not in want.

No one had even considered he might not wish to see them.

Now Abby wondered. If this wealthy man was their father, would he, like Dev, think they were after his money?

She shivered despite the warm evening. How awful for people to suspect others couldn't like you for yourself, but only because of your money.

Or family position--her grandmother's view of life.

Maybe Abby could verify the relationship and slip away without saying anything. She'd report back to Caroline and Michelle and the three of them could decide what to do next.

Abby ordered pizza, picked up the gardening book she'd purchased that morning and sat in the only easy chair in the apartment. *Step-by-Step to a Perfect Garden* seemed as basic as she could get. Beginning at the beginning she soaked up all the advice the book gave.

She was well into the book when the knock came on the door.

The pizza. About time, she was starving. Putting down the book, she grabbed her purse and hurried to the door. Opening it, she was astonished to see Dev standing there-- holding a pizza box.

"Pizza delivery," he said easily. Without waiting for an invitation, he stepped inside.

Abby looked out to the driveway. Only Dev's car was visible.

"How did you get the pizza?" she asked, slowly closing the door behind her. He'd already gone into the tiny kitchen.

"Met the guy just as I was pulling in. Thought maybe you'd take pity on a hardworking man and offer to share." He stood in the doorway. "Especially since I paid for it."

"I'll pay you back," she said, reaching for her wallet.

"You don't want to share?"

Abby had spent all day planning how she'd casually ask him to join her for dinner. She almost laughed aloud at his question. Feigning indifference, she shrugged.

"It's fine with me. But you didn't get a chance to choose toppings."

"I peeked. Looks great. I'm not sure it'll be enough for both of us, but we can order a second one if we want."

"I didn't expect company," she said, laying down her purse and heading for the kitchen. "If I had known you would be home, I'd have ordered a larger one."

She grabbed plates, napkins and glasses. Dev pulled a pitcher of iced tea from the refrigerator. Just as if he'd been doing it forever, she thought as she set the small table against the wall.

"Did you just finish work this late?" she asked when they were seated.

He'd discarded his suit jacket somewhere, loosened his tie and rolled back the sleeves of his shirt, revealing muscular arms. His dark hair was mussed, as if he'd run his fingers through it in frustration.

Abby didn't like the way her body began to react around him. She was here on a mission, not to fall for some sexy Texan.

"I feel I'm doing two jobs with Dad out. I had some department managers in this afternoon for a planning session. It ran late."

He looked at her, his eyes silvery in the light. "Actually, this is the second day I've left early since Dad's been out."

Blood thundered in her veins. Dev didn't say it, but she knew he meant he'd left early because of her.

"Oh."

Slowly he smiled and Abby felt her insides begin to melt.

Chapter Three

Flustered, Abby didn't like the feeling. She needed to be in complete control so she'd give nothing away!

"So, your father will be home soon, and then you'll just have your own job to do, right?"

"He'll be home soon, but I'm not sure when he'll be back to a full load at the office."

"He was ill, I think you said." Had Dev mentioned it? Or had it been the secretary who had told her that? "Nothing life-threatening, I hope."

"Appendicitis with complications. Including being a bit rundown due to stress. He'll be fine."

The pizza was good and Abby had no trouble eating her share. If Dev didn't want to talk, she wasn't going to fill the silence. Too aware of where her tongue could lead her, she knew discretion was the better path for her.

"If you didn't want me to crash dinner, you could have said so," he said a few moments later.

She met his gaze, trying to ignore the rampant sensations that filled her with just a look from the man. What would happen if he touched her again? Caught her close and kissed her?

Heat washed through her and she knew her skin flushed. She'd give anything to be impervious to such reactions. Her fair skin was the bane of her existence. She had to remember he was her new employer--nothing more.

No kisses!

"I'm glad to have you here," she said primly.

"But?"

She shook her head and smiled. "But nothing. I'm just not sure what to say." What to say that wouldn't give her away.

"Then tell me about swimming in the middle of the night," he suggested, amusement dancing in his eyes.

"I didn't expect to be caught out," she said, laughing softly. "I just couldn't resist. And if I hadn't forgotten the towel, you'd have never known."

"Makes me wonder what else goes on around here that I don't know about," he said easily.

Guilt had her dropping her gaze to her pizza. They were down to the last piece. Would Dev leave as soon as he ate or stay a bit longer? What did she want him to do?

"Do you want a blow-by-blow account of my day?" Abby asked playfully.

"I don't think I need it. I can see a difference in the yard's appearance already. Keep it up and the place will be perfect when Mom and Dad return."

An unexpected feeling of satisfaction spread through her at his words. She'd done very little, actually more afraid of messing up than helping. But some of the shaggy appearance of the flowers had disappeared when she cut the dead blossoms. And with the grass taken care of, the entire estate looked better--even she acknowledged that. Thank goodness the rider-mower was so easy to use--once she'd figured out how to steer it!

"Did you have enough or should I order more?" Dev asked when he finished the last piece of pizza.

"I'm full. You're the one who could probably use more," Abby replied.

"It'll hold me for a while."

"Thanks for buying it," she said shyly.

He shrugged. "Actually, I called you a couple of times today. I was going to ask you out to dinner--my turn after last night."

"Oh. I was outside working."

She just hoped he didn't expect to see miraculous improvement in the yard after all her supposed hours working!

"Maybe you should carry a cell phone so people can reach you during the day."

"I do. Shall I give you the number?" She thought about it for a moment, worried it had the area code for New Orleans. Well, he knew she'd been there, so hopefully he wouldn't think a thing of her having that number.

"I should have known. You'd want to know if your sister calls to say the baby's coming."

"Caroline? She couldn't--" Almost too late Abby realized the pitfall. Caroline didn't know where she was, or what she was doing. She thought Abby was taking a few days of vacation to visit with friends.

"Couldn't?"

"*Wouldn't* call me uh, anytime soon. The baby isn't due until the second week in November."

"Her first?"

"She was pregnant before and miscarried. We're trying to make sure she delivers a healthy baby this time."

"Are you a doctor?" Dev joked. "How are you making sure she delivers a healthy baby?"

"Mostly by making sure she hasn't a thing to worry about," Abby said, standing.

She needed to change the subject.

"I found some strawberries in that plot behind the shrubbery on the far side of the pool. Want some with ice cream?" she asked, reaching for his plate.

His hand circled her wrist, holding her in place. "Swiping produce now?"

Her heart tripping double time, Abby could scarcely breathe. His touch wreaked havoc with her senses. His hand was warm and firm, his fingers stroking her lightly, but the shivering sensations that danced on her skin was disturbing and tantalizing. Gazing into his silvery eyes, Abby longed to drop the plate and move closer.

Forgotten was the need for secrecy, for subterfuge. For one crazy moment she wanted to explore the excitement of being with Dev Hamilton.

When his thumb brushed lightly against the soft inner skin of her arm, Abby knew she was going to blow everything if she didn't put some distance between them.

Tugging her wrist free, she stepped back.

"I didn't want them to go to waste," she said breathlessly. "With no one else around, I didn't think you'd mind.," Get a grip, she told herself as she stepped into the minuscule kitchen.

"You're right, I don't. Glad they can be enjoyed. Can I help?" Dev was right behind her. She imagined she could feel the warmth from his body encase her. The kitchen wasn't big enough for two people to move around without bumping into each other.

"No, I'm fine. I can manage."

He reached around her and opened the cupboard door, taking down two bowls. Once again Abby was struck with how they worked together as if choreographed.

She withdrew the ice cream from the freezer and Dev took it from her hands. In only a moment, he had scooped servings into two bowls. She produced the sliced strawberries.

"Want to take them out to the pool?" he asked.

"No. Let's just sit inside." And when he was done, maybe he'd leave and let her get herself under control!

"Want coffee?" she asked.

"I'd take some more iced tea," he said heading for the living room.

Grateful for something to do, Abby fixed them both fresh glasses.

"What's this?" Dev asked when she entered the room a few minutes later. In his hand was the gardening book she'd been reading.

Stunned, Abby stared at it. Endless seconds later she

looked at Dev. His expression gave nothing away. He must be great in business, she thought wildly, nothing escaped his notice.

Frantically, she tried to think. Placing his glass near him, she took hers to the chair opposite. He'd set her ice cream bowl near him, but she couldn't sit that close. Reaching for it she tried smiling. Would her cheeks crack?

"I, um, was a, ah, contributor to the book. I got a copy to see how things turned out."

"I'm impressed. Which part was yours?"

"Which part?" Abby scrambled for an idea. Staring at the book, her mind went blank.

"Did you do a chapter or something?" Dev asked, watching her oddly.

"Oh, no. I worked with one of the writers on several sections. That's all."

He glanced at the spine. "You aren't listed."

"No. Umm, I sort of researched things for one of the authors. Suggested the outline of the section on, uh, annuals." She trailed off, not having any idea what she was talking about. Was there a section on annuals in that particular book? She hoped so.

"Do you do this kind of thing often?"

"No. I prefer to work outside. Anyway, it's done now and I doubt I'll collaborate on any other books."

"How did it turn out?"

"What?"

"Your input to the book."

"I just started reading it. So far so good."

Smiling inanely, Abby longed to change the subject. What would be compelling enough to get him off the subject of the blasted book! If she'd suspected he was planning to drop by, she'd have hidden it beneath the pillow in her bedroom. The last thing she needed was for Dev to see her reading a gardener's book for beginners.

Dev put the book down and picked up his ice cream again. "So, planning any more midnight swims?"

Abby wanted to close her eyes and sink through the floor. Maybe his visit could end soon. The book was bad enough, now he was reminding her of that. She couldn't forget his offer to join her if she went again.

"No." She took a spoonful of ice cream.

"Let me know when you get your bathing suit, we can use the pool one evening."

"Ump."

When pigs fly. There was no way she was going to tell him she'd bought a swimsuit today. She was already too aware of the man. The last thing she needed was to see him in swim trunks.

Abby had a working knowledge of the human body from all her anatomy classes. Which only aided her in imagining Dev in a swimsuit. With his broad shoulders and muscular built, she bet he was a knockout. He was gorgeous enough in business attire. She didn't think she should get within fifty feet of him without his clothes.

But the image danced before her eyes, tempting her to agree.

She cleared her throat. "So the rest of the staff returns tomorrow?" she asked.

"Yes. Mrs. Mitton is the housekeeper. She lives in. Thelma Fields is the cook. You'll love her food. She cooks for the entire household, so if you want, you can have your meals there. Mrs. Mitton has a couple of women in during the week to help with the laundry and housework."

"I look forward to meeting them," she said politely.

The amusement danced in his eyes again.

"Did I say something funny?" she asked, puzzled.

"Sometimes you sound like some prissy debutante. Other times you're open and forthright. And yet, I detect a hint of something mysterious about you, Abby Brown. Who are you really?"

"My grandmother drilled good manners into us." She didn't want to touch the subject of who she was. He'd have a fit if he found out. She couldn't let that happen.

"She did a good job. You are an intriguing woman."

Oh gosh, the last thing she needed was him to become interested in learning more about her. She needed space.

"If you're finished, I'll take your bowl," she said, jumping to her feet, torn between wanting to spend time with Dev because he was the most attractive man she'd ever met, and the need to get him out before the conversation took another personal turn.

"In a hurry for me to leave?" he asked, rising.

"Not at all. But I'm sure you have things to do. I'm surprised you don't have a date tonight. I can't expect to monopolize your time. Thanks for stopping by and for the pizza and everything."

Dev ran his hand around the back of his neck, then

stretched. Abby watched, fascinated, wishing suddenly she had taken him up on the swimming offer.

"No date tonight," he said shortly. "I enjoyed the pizza and the ice cream."

"Thank you. You bought it."

"So I did." He took a step closer. "So if I bought dinner, maybe *this* was my date for tonight."

She couldn't move. Clenching the bowls tightly in her hands, she wanted to dash away and contrarily at the same time, step closer.

"Short date."

"Fun, too." Slowly he leaned closer until his face filled her vision.

He was going to kiss her and Abby didn't know what to do. Frantically she tried to decide what would be the better plan--give in, or run away. Taking too long, she ended up doing nothing except slowly letting her eyes close.

The touch of his lips was wonderful. Warm and firm, they moved against hers in a kiss that zapped her knees and made it difficult for her to stand. *Don't drop the bowls*, was the only thought that filtered through the raging delight that consumed her.

All too soon, he stepped back.

"If you change your mind about swimming later, let me know. My room's the corner one in the back."

With that he left.

Abby stared after him in a bemused trance for several minutes. Her lips still felt the pressure of his. Her heart raced and danced. Her hands grew numb clenching the ice cream bowls. Blinking, she gradually became aware of standing in the empty living room.

Had he really kissed her?

Smiling, she almost waltzed into the kitchen.

He had, and she liked it! Oh, oh. She was in trouble now.

Dev grabbed his briefcase and suit jacket from the car. He glanced at the garage apartment once more before heading for the main house, his senses on alert. Something was odd about Abby Brown. Odd and fascinating. She was a contradiction that he didn't understand--yet.

He strode across the yard, noticing the changes she'd wrought. At least she was making a start. He hoped the grounds were back in order by the time his mother saw them.

As he skirted the pool, he remembered finding the towel that morning and knowing Abby had gone swimming alone. For a moment, the image of her sleek body moving through the water had strengthened his resolve to get to know her better.

He was wary around women who played games. More often than not, a woman wanted to be seen with him, to enhance her own status in the world. He was generous, liked to have a good time and didn't mind being used as a status symbol. But he wasn't planning to settle down with anyone who was nothing more than a fortune hunter. After all, his near brush with matrimony with his former fiancée had taught him that lesson.

Not that he was thinking about marriage--just a few

evenings in the company of Abby Brown. She intrigued him-
-shy one moment, funny the next, with interesting odd slants
on things. There was more to her than he at first suspected.

Dev unlocked the door to the kitchen and entered.
Walking through to the study, he placed the day's mail in the
growing pile, and set his briefcase on the floor beside the
desk. Tomorrow, he'd work from the study to make sure he
was home when Mrs. Mitton returned. And Thelma. Both
women had been given paid vacations while his stepfather
and mother took that cruise.

Dev hoped the extended trip had worked as his mother
wanted and that Samuel was returning in much improved
health. Dev had done his best to shelter him from
everything--to enable him to devote his full energy toward
recovery.

Taking the stairs two at a time, Dev headed for his
room. Too early to go to bed, but not too early to change
and head for the pool.

Would she come tonight despite her statement to the
contrary? Or would he wait in vain?

The water felt good. He enjoyed swimming. He should
make time for it more often.

Once he was tired of swimming, he lay back in one of
the lounge chairs, letting the warmth of the evening
evaporate the water.

Dev awoke, immediately alert. He lay on one of the
lounge chairs near the pool. The pool light that was no
longer on, he noticed. Glancing at his watch, he saw it was
after one. The night was dark, clouds drifted across the stars,

throwing moving shadows across the lawn, the surface of the water.

He rubbed his face. She wasn't coming after all. Just as she'd said. He might as well take a final dip and head for bed. He'd been so sure she'd show up.

Just then he heard the swish of someone walking on the grass.

Abby stepped onto the cool concrete surrounding the pool and hesitated. Dev could barely see her outlined against the night stars. She seemed to peer toward the house.

She dropped a towel on a chair and pulled her T-shirt over her head. For a moment he held his breath.

Then a cloud blotted the faint light and she was lost to sight, just a vague silhouette against the sky.

When she plunged into the water, Dev remembered his warning that she should not go swimming alone. How hypocritical. He'd gone swimming alone.

Still, why hadn't she called him?

Because she wasn't out to entice him. She said what she felt, and she hadn't wanted him here.

Tough. He rose and touched the switch that turned on the underwater pool lights.

Abby shot straight to the surface.

"Oh my gosh, you scared me half to death!" Her voice was almost a yell when she saw him at the edge. Treading water, she slicked back her hair and glared at him.

"You can see better with the lights on," he said mildly.

"I was doing fine."

Dev made a shallow dive, surfacing right in front of her.

"I see your clothes arrived?"

"You said I could use the pool." Treading water, she moved back a few feet. Dev followed.

"I'm not complaining about that, but about your swimming alone."

"Okay. I'm not alone now," she said, kicking back and starting to swim again. Dev paced her as they moved up and down the long pool. She was serious about swimming and he enjoyed the workout. Hadn't she said she wanted to relax her muscles? It worked with his own as well.

Stopping at last, Abby climbed out of the shallow end.

"Don't go yet," Dev said, standing beside her. For a moment he felt her gaze on his chest. Enjoyed the way her eyes widened as she studied him. When she looked away, he wanted her to look back. Crazy.

"Abby?"

"I've got to go now. Thanks for the swim."

Not even thinking, just reacting, Dev reached for her before she could leave. He pulled her cool body into his arms, holding her firmly enough to mold her soft form against his harder one. Her lips were cool, initially. But after his moved against hers, they warmed.

Softly he traced her curves, feeling the edge of her suit, the silky texture of her back. The wet strands of her hair tangled with his fingers. Deepening the kiss, Dev was unaware of time drifting by. Her body seemed a perfect match to his and her kisses inflamed him. The touch of her hands against his shoulders, his chest ignited a conflagration that the pool water couldn't extinguish.

When she pushed against him, he reluctantly released

her.

"I don't think that was a great idea," she said, sloshing through the water to the shallow steps in the corner.

"Why not?"

"You're too dangerous," she muttered, rising from the pool, water streaming from her.

Dev stood still, glad the water covered his body's reaction to her. She found him *dangerous*? Then he smiled. He knew she didn't mean in a threatening manner. At least not threatening in a physical sense.

"Care to clarify that?"

She stopped drying her hair with the towel and looked at him.

"As if you needed any clarification. You probably have women dropping like flies at your feet."

Dev roared with laughter. "Such an appealing picture. Flies?"

"You know what I mean," she snapped. Wrapping the towel around her waist, she yanked on her T-shirt.

He vaulted from the side of the pool and walked over to her before she could leave. Away from the pool, the light was fainter. But he could see her clearly enough to recognize the wariness with which she regarded him.

"It was just a kiss, Abby."

"Yes, I know. And I want to keep it at just a kiss. Good night, Dev." She turned and hurried into the dark yard.

"Here's the game plan," Abby muttered to herself as she almost ran to her apartment. "Do all you can to find out about Samuel Williams, and stay as far away from Dev as you can!"

She glanced over her shoulder. "And no more kisses," she whispered, wondering if she'd be able to resist if he offered more.

First thing Saturday morning, Abby skimmed as much of the gardening book as she could. Before going swimming the previous night, she'd read several chapters. She now had a nodding acquaintance with gardening in this zone and if she could just hold on and appear to be doing something until the Williams' returned home, she'd be set.

Dressed in loose shorts and a light cotton top, she headed outside. She'd seen a station wagon arrive some time ago. One of the household staff members, she bet. When the old car had shown up, she knew she should go and introduce herself. Maybe once everyone was in place, Dev would remember she worked for his father and establish some boundaries. After all she was the hired help. Shouldn't he keep his distance?

No such luck today. He was lounging against the counter in the kitchen chatting with the two older women when Abby knocked on the door. Within ten minutes, all four sat around the kitchen table like old friends. Thelma had brought fresh-baked cookies with her.

"Knowing I wouldn't have time to bake any before someone demanded something sweet to eat, I brought them from home," she said, smiling at Dev.

"I missed your cooking," he said with a shrug, reaching for another cookie.

Abby watched, fascinated. For a moment she imagined

him as a teenager, mischievous and charming, able to wrap the cook around his little finger.

"As if you come to visit often enough to enjoy it," Thelma said.

"I may be here more than you think the next few weeks," he said, glancing at Abby.

She tried to ignore him. Hadn't she vowed to keep her distance just a few hours ago?

"How do you like it here?" Mrs. Mitton asked Abby.

"So far so good. The yard is lovely or will be soon. And the apartment's great."

"Now don't go fixing your own meals when you can eat with us," Thelma said.

Abby smiled, knowing she wouldn't be here long enough to establish any routine.

"Abby's promised to make sure there're plenty of flowers in the house when Mom gets home," Dev said, as if challenging her to ignore him any longer.

She nodded. "If you tell me which rooms you'd like arrangements in, I'll see to it," she said, addressing Mrs. Mitton.

Before that woman could respond, Dev stood.

"Come with me, Abby. I'll give you a grand tour. That way you can see which color combinations and flowers would work in each room."

He held out his hand, but she ignored it--wishing she could ignore the hint of command behind his suggestion.

Mrs. Mitton looked surprised, then she exchanged glances with Thelma. Both smiled.

Abby wanted to make it perfectly clear that nothing was

going on, but she dare not argue against something that hadn't been voiced.

"Mrs. Mitton could show me," she said a minute later when Dev led the way down the wide hallway to the open foyer.

"Ah, but this is my home, I can show you so much better, don't you think?"

"I thought this was your stepfather's home."

He hesitated a moment and studied her with narrowed eyes. "It belongs to him, but it's my home, too."

Abby looked around. The foyer was large, with a curving stairway that led to the second story. Through a wide archway, she saw the elegant living room. Cream and gold and blue were the dominant colors. She stepped to the arch and admired the decor. While it was sumptuous, it was also inviting. Welcoming. So unlike the formal parlor in her grandmother's house.

Dev led her into the room, pointing out locations he knew his mother liked flowers. Next came the dining room.

"And that room?" Abby asked in passing at the door, partially ajar.

"That's Dad's study."

"Does he like flowers? I could do an arrangement for that room as well," she said, wishing she could glimpse inside.

Would there be old records, letters, something to tie Dev's father to the Sam Williams who had once married Amanda Talmadge and been forced to abandon his family twenty-three years ago?

Chapter Four

"**N**o need for flowers in there--it's a working office." Dev touched her shoulder lightly, urging her into the dining room.

It was a spacious, elegant room with a stately table which would seat twelve centered beneath a huge crystal chandelier. The rich cherry wood gleamed. Had Mrs. Mitton begun working already or was the house kept in excellent condition despite the housekeeper's absence?

"How long ago did your father become ill?" she asked, touching the satiny finish.

"Several weeks, why?"

"The house is immaculate. I wondered how long Mrs. Mitton had been gone."

"The staff was given a three-week vacation when my parents left for their cruise. Don't you think I've been dusting and keeping things up?" he asked. A gleam in his eyes told her he was teasing.

Abby laughed and shook her head. "Nope. Never for one minute."

He frowned. "How can you say that? I could have worked my fingers to the bone every night after work."

"I can see you ordering minions about, but not participating in such mundane tasks."

"I keep my own place tidy--but I do have a cleaning service which comes in once a week."

"See, a single person doesn't mess up their own place enough to need a service."

"Maybe *need* is strong, maybe it's just that I like having it."

And can indulge yourself, she thought, looking away before she said something inappropriate. Why not? Truth to tell if she made enough money, she'd probably indulge herself by having someone come in once a week, too.

Not that it took that much effort to dust and vacuum her small apartment, but still, the luxury of having someone else do it was appealing.

"My mother likes big bouquets on the sideboard. Roses are her favorite."

"So you said," Abby murmured, studying the antique furniture. She'd love to see quantities of fragrant blossoms add their color to the room. She'd also love to see the room filled with guests, laughing, enjoying Thelma's cooking, and sharing amusing anecdotes of their lives.

"So what else?" she asked briskly, damping down her imagination. She wouldn't be here long enough to even glimpse a party through the window, much less attend one. Once she had her answer, she'd be gone.

Glancing at Dev, she frowned. For some reason the thought of leaving was disquieting.

"The small sun room." Dev led the way. "My mother

spends a lot of time here. Of course with all the glass, she can see much of the garden already."

He paused in the doorway. Abby peeked around him. White wicker furniture was scattered in a casual array. The solid glass walls seemed to bring the outdoors in, making it a part of the room.

She saw the spot where she'd mowed down the flowers and winced. She had to get something to replace the ones she'd ruined before his mother arrived. It might be better to wait for Friday so if in transplanting the flowers from the pots to the ground she did something wrong and they died, she would be gone before it became noticeable.

"There's a sitting room upstairs off the master bedroom which my mother uses a lot--to read or write letters. A small vase up there would be nice."

Abby went on alert. A room right off the master bedroom? How perfect. She now had a reason to be in all parts of the house for the search Josh suggested.

"Can I see that, too?" she asked, hoping her excitement didn't show.

"Sure." Dev led the way up the curving stairs. He turned left at the top and opened a door into a beautiful, feminine room. The white lacy curtains on the windows were sparkling and crisp. The damask rose-colored chaise-lounge invited someone to recline, read, or just daydream. The Queen Anne furniture added to the romantic setting--lovely and delicate.

Abby gazed around the room. A strong yearning filled

her. She'd love to have a room like this where she could retreat and recharge.

Through an open door, she glimpsed a bed--the master bedroom.

"Where's your bedroom?" she asked, turning to face him. "Now that we're on this level, I might as well see everything, right?"

She couldn't explain her curiosity. Dev would provide nothing she needed to further her quest, but that didn't stop her from being interested in everything about the man.

"Across and down the hall. But I warn you, no flowers. The room still looks like it did when I left for college. I don't stay here often enough to change it."

He pushed open a door to the room a minute later.

Abby smiled when she stepped in. It looked like a teenager's room. Posters of racing cars and pop musicians hung on the wall. Notebooks were stacked haphazardly on crowded shelves. She walked over to study the trophies on one shelf--all for swimming events.

"I ought to clear it out and start over," he said from the doorway.

Abby looked over her shoulder. He leaned against the frame, his hands in his pockets, surveying the room with wry amusement.

"Why? It's like a museum piece, a slice of history."

"Ouch, I'm not that old."

"How old?" she asked. She could appease a tiny segment of her curiosity.

"Twenty-seven on my next birthday. Not much older than you."

Abby opened her mouth to refute that, then snapped it shut. Of course, he thought she was twenty-six. A narrow escape. Smiling wanly, she turned away, looking at the scraps of papers pinned to a cork board. What had been important to Dev Hamilton as a teenager?

Dev glanced at his watch. "If I know Thelma, lunch will be waiting."

Abby nodded and continued to prowl around his room.

The thought crossed his mind he could shut the door and no one would disturb them.

Yet, despite the kisses they'd shared, he was unsure if Abby would stand to have the door closed. She confused him and intrigued him.

Her long legs were tanned beneath her shorts. The loose top she wore might have been for camouflage, except when she moved, it clung to her body, revealing her high breasts and the gentle curve of her waist.

He remembered how she'd appeared in her swimsuit in the starlight.

And the growing awareness seemed all the stronger for the memory.

"Let's go," he said abruptly. He wasn't interested in a relationship. He had work that kept him busy. And a small circle of select friends he knew liked him for who he was, not for what he had.

"Thanks for letting me see your room. It's different from mine as a kid. My grandmother insisted it be decorated for a young girl, but I was never allowed to have a single toy out of place except when I was playing with it, or a single book not properly placed on its shelf when I finished reading. I wish I could have hung up posters," she said wistfully as she passed him.

Dev inhaled her fragrance, sweet and light--touching him deep inside like nothing else ever had.

He wanted to pull her into his arms and kiss her. To feel the soft curves of her body against him as he had last night. Explore the burning attraction that grew each moment, until he could put out the flame and move on.

Abby ran lightly down the stairs. "Thanks for the tour."

"Wait." He followed, catching up when they reached the ground level. His hand grabbed her arm, stopping her precipitous flight, swinging her around to face him.

"Where are you going?"

"To my apartment. I have an idea of the kind of flowers to make into arrangements. I'll have them ready the day your parents return. No problem. So I'm done, right?"

"Stay for lunch."

Slowly the impression of her soft skin filtered to his mind. He wanted to rub his fingertips against the silky texture and absorb the sensations. Holding his impulse in check, going against his strong inclination, he released her.

"Oh, I couldn't do that."

"Thelma will have prepared enough for an army. I know her."

She seemed torn. Dev watched the expressions chase

across her face and almost laughed when she reluctantly accepted.

Why the reluctance? he wondered.

That was part of the mystery. Sometimes she seemed to enjoy being with him, other times she looked as if she wanted to be anywhere else.

True to Dev's forecast, Thelma had cold chicken salad, hot rolls and tossed fruit ready for lunch--enough for everyone.

"I thought you and Abby could eat on the patio. It's nice out and you should take advantage of the weather before it becomes too hot," she said. "Mrs. Mitton has already set a table out there."

"Oh, I thought we'd all eat in here," Abby said.

Had Thelma forgotten Abby was also an employee of the estate? She should eat with the rest of the staff. Besides, the longer she spent with Dev, the more difficult it became to remember why she was in Houston.

She should be searching for information about her father, not spending the day with Dev Hamilton.

But in the end, Abby complied.

The patio was on the side of the house by the dining room. The flagstone was swept and tidy. She'd trimmed the grass around it herself when making sweeps with the riding mower. There were hanging baskets from the lattice cover, the plants drooping in the heat.

Was she supposed to water them, she thought, stricken. They looked like they were dying.

The grass and flower beds were on automatic sprinklers. She'd never thought about looking for pots and planters.

After Dev left, she'd come back and see about giving them some water.

Which reminded her, when would Dev be leaving?

She wanted to get inside the house to search for anything that might establish Samuel Williams' identity, and for that she needed free access. Which she wasn't sure she'd get with Mrs. Mitton, but knew for certain she wouldn't get with Dev around. Didn't he have other plans for the weekend?

Lunch was delicious. Abby wished she could have enjoyed it, but she felt edgy--too conscious of Dev sitting at her right. If she moved her leg a bit, she'd bump his knee. She felt the warmth from his leg. Trying to ignore the sensations that built, she focused on eating. Maybe she could finish quickly and escape.

"Tell me more about Abby Brown," Dev invited. "Beyond what's on your résumé and that you have a pregnant sister living nearby who will be delivering in November."

Had she told him Caroline's delivery date? She had to watch it, she didn't want to give too much away. But what was the harm?

Normally she was open and friendly. She'd think nothing about telling new friends about her life. The danger with Dev was to safely do so without revealing who she really was.

He seemed genuinely interested. And she admitted to

being flattered. Was he as curious about her as she was about him?

"Start easy, then," he said after the silence ran on for several minutes. "What's your favorite flower?" He watched her as she scanned the yard.

"Roses," she said promptly.

She had to cut him off. The longer they spent together, the more they talked, the greater the chance he'd discover her secret. And then she'd probably be out on her ear so fast she wouldn't know which end was up.

"Floribunda, tea, climbing, which?"

Staring at him, her mind went blank. What was he talking about? Roses?

"Umm, any as long as they're red," she said, taking a large bite of salad, hoping he wouldn't expect her to talk with her mouth full. How long could she stall that way? There was only so much salad left in the serving bowl and she had already eaten a fair amount. But anything was better than running the risk of exposure.

"Tell me Dev, do you often eat with the hired help?" she said, when she could speak again, hoping to change the subject.

His gazed narrowed. "What do you mean by that?"

She waved her hand around the patio. "My grandmother would never have sat down with--" Too late. Good grief, she was absolutely no good at this undercover work.

At his sharp look, she tried to recover. "I mean, I work for you. Should you be eating with me? Should I be here?"

"Have you been reading *Jane Eyre*? I'm not some lord of

the manor, Abby. And technically, you work for my parents. I facilitated the hiring process, but that's all. Today's your day off, right?"

She nodded, taking a breath, trying to calm her roiling senses. Remembering what happened between Mr. Rochester and his hired governess, she blinked. Listening to Dev, she tried to focus, but images of last night by the pool kept interfering.

He'd kissed her and she'd kissed him back. Today she'd been wary around him, trying to keep out of his way. But he'd given no indication that he wanted to touch her, kiss her or take this tenuous interaction any further.

Except for that hot kiss, nothing in his actions had been exceptional for a man dealing with an employee.

He looked at her.

"What?" Had he been talking while her mind wandered?

"I said, I often have lunch with colleagues at work. Is this any different?"

"No, I guess not. Except we're not talking business."

"I did ask what flowers you liked."

She nodded, trying to relax. He'd been perfectly reasonable. It was her own conscience that was causing the problems.

For a second, she debated taking him into her confidence. Surely by now he'd know she wasn't some gold-digger after his stepfather's money. If she could just get him to listen to her story, maybe he'd be able to answer her questions.

Then she remembered his saying Samuel Williams had

never lived in Mississippi. But Dev had only known the man for the last ten years or so. If Sam Williams thought he was still evading a murder warrant, would he tell his young stepson or even his wife? And as the years progressed, when would he say, Oh, by the way, I'm wanted on a murder charge in Mississippi?

"You intrigue me," Dev said.

Abby looked into his eyes, startled by the words.

"Me? Why?"

"Let's just say you're different from other women I know."

She frowned. What was he saying? "We're just having lunch."

"That's what I mean. Anyone else would preen and immediately think that I was suggesting something more than lunch. You're the opposite. You try to deny there's anything between us. And I think we both know there is something."

"Right now it's lunch between us."

He nodded. "But after last night, a woman might be excused for suspecting there's more."

"Oh, the kiss." That wonderful, sexy, heat-inducing kiss that had about knocked her off her feet.

He nodded again.

"Well, people exchange kisses all the time. It doesn't have to mean anything. Right?"

She needed some confirmation here. Something that would end the daydreams if she would let herself think about that kiss more than one second at a time.

"And sometimes kissing does mean something."

"Well, sure, between a man and a woman who have a mutual attraction for each other."

"As we do not?"

Abby shook her head, her eyes firmly fixed on her salad. This conversation was getting out of hand. She couldn't continue to deny the attraction she felt for Dev much longer. If she did, he'd begin to suspect she was protesting too much. But she couldn't let herself be sidetracked--no matter how tantalizing the distraction.

She was on a quest and it didn't include falling for Dev Hamilton!

"Liar," he said softly, teasingly.

She looked up, shocked. Did he suspect--

No, he was flirting with her. He didn't believe her assertion that she was uninterested. Was he daring her to admit to the attraction that shimmered between them?

"I think you're too used to women throwing themselves at you," she said primly.

"Ah, the flies at my feet."

Heat flushed through her but she refused to give in to embarrassment. "That's right. And I'm sorry to disappoint you, but I won't be one of them."

"Wanna bet?" he said softly, leaning closer.

His breath fanned against her cheek and she wanted to follow suit. Lean closer. Until their lips touched.

Heat spiraled through her as she met his gaze, held it as long as she could. The shimmering sensations that invaded every cell held her enthralled. Would another kiss hurt?

"Is that some sort of challenge?" she asked, placing her fork on her plate and sitting up straight as if prepared to do battle.

He sprawled back in his chair, stretching out his legs, brushing hers in the process. Slowly he smiled. "Could be."

Abby jumped up, pushing back her chair. "I'm here to take care of the garden, Mr. Hamilton, not flirt with the estate owners' son."

She started to turn, had a second thought and reached out to grab another couple of Thelma's heavenly baking powder biscuits. She stormed across the yard. Hearing Dev's mocking laughter behind her, she tossed her head and kept walking. That man was as arrogant as any of the young doctors that strutted through the halls of the hospital.

Maybe it was time he realized not every woman swooned at his feet. Though she was hard pressed to imagine anyone trying to resist. Especially herself.

It was late in the afternoon when she heard his sports car. Peering between the slats of the blinds in her window, she watched as he put down the top, and prepared to leave. Just before backing out of the long driveway, he looked up-- directly into her eyes.

Only he couldn't see her, could he?

From his audacious wave, she suspected he could.

Darn! She could almost hear his laughter. And knew the point had gone to him.

It was odd to think the day had become flat, just because he'd left.

She'd been on her own since leaving the lunch table. But

it was only when he left the estate that she felt lonely. Maybe she should go up to the house and talk with Mrs. Mitton or Thelma.

Or maybe she needed to read more of the gardening book before Monday so she had some idea of how to spend her time during the coming week. If only Samuel Williams would come home early. She'd talk to him, resolve the situation one way or the other and be on her way back to New Orleans.

Late the next morning, Abby garnered her courage and headed for the main house. She considered today was the best day to try Josh's plan to look for clues into the history of this Sam Williams.

Dev hadn't returned yesterday. Abby ignored the pang that knowledge brought. Had he taken someone else out? Stayed the night?

Not that she cared. He could do whatever he wanted.

But it had been late when she at last fell asleep. Her first action this morning had been to peek through the blinds to look for his car.

Turning away from the empty driveway, she tried to focus on her quest.

She'd tell Mrs. Mitton she needed to see the rooms again. Hopefully the housekeeper wouldn't accompany her. Hadn't Dev vouched for her?

It was almost too easy, Abby thought a few minutes later as she walked alone into the foyer. The warm welcome from both Mrs. Mitton and Thelma made her feel guilty about her deception. Their generous trusting natures pricked her conscience.

When she stood in the doorway to the study, however, Abby realized she wouldn't be able to delve into secret places. Josh might be able to search a person's home when in the course of some investigation, but she couldn't do it.

She'd been raised by a strict woman who had definite ideas about privacy and that much, at least, had rubbed off on Abby.

She roamed around the room, touching the desk, the chair behind it. One wall was lined with bookshelves filled with an eclectic assortment of books. She scanned the titles, touching one every so often when she recognized one she'd read. He seemed to like mysteries, as did she. Did that suggest a tie?

Sitting in one of the wing-back chairs that flanked a wide table, she wondered what Dev liked. What books he enjoyed. Did he spend a lot of time in here?

The room reflected a man's taste. There were no curtains on the windows, just wooden blinds--opened now, as were the windows, to let in the sunshine and fresh air. The room had a similar view as the sun-room, she noted, the bare patch where she'd eradicated the flowers still glaringly obvious.

Abby didn't know how much time passed, until suddenly she heard Dev's voice. He was in the house, calling for her! Mrs. Mitton must have told him she was here.

Jumping to her feet, Abby crossed the room silently, heading for the door. Could she get to the living room before he saw her? She had no business being in his father's office. He'd be furious if he discovered her here. And maybe suspicious.

He was already in the foyer.

Looking around frantically, she spied the window. Dashing across the room, she looked down. It wasn't a far drop into a flower bed with the soft dirt. The chances of getting hurt were minimal. Without another thought, she sat on the sill, pushed away the hinged screen, swung her legs out and jumped.

"Oof." The landing was harder than she expected. The screen slammed against the window frame, trembled a moment, then stayed in place. Dropping to her knees, she hugged the house, crouching by the wall, hoping Dev hadn't seen her as she dropped out of sight. Praying he'd go away long enough for her to dash across the yard and get back to her apartment.

She counted the seconds as they ticked by and nothing happened. Abby began to relax. That was close, but at least she escaped. She leaned forward on her knees, the dirt cool and slightly damp against her skin. Crawling toward the grass, she moved slowly, quietly, cautiously.

"Abby?"

Darn! Slowly she sank back on her feet, and looked over her shoulder at Dev. Framed in the window, he gazed back at her.

"What are you doing?"

Trying to get away from you before you suspect more than you should, she thought, searching frantically for an answer. "I saw some, uh, weeds. *E varicose*, you know? I can't stand to have them mess up a flower garden." Slowly, using her body to shield her hand from his sight, she pulled up a plant.

Had he seen her go through the window?

"Mrs. Mitton said you'd been in the house a while ago. I called, but I guess you'd already left."

"Umm." Slowly Abby stood, brushing the dirt from her knees. "I, uh, wanted to see the living room again to see what flowers would work. I didn't need long to do that."

"I don't expect you to work on Sundays."

"Right. I was just walking by and saw the weeds," she said, holding out the dangling plant. She hoped it wasn't some rare flower that couldn't be replaced.

"And couldn't resist?" Was there mockery in his voice?

She shrugged, stepped out of the flower bed and turned toward the garage. "I'll wait until tomorrow, then."

"Want to go to the beach?" Dev asked as Abby took a step away.

She looked at him over her shoulder, turning slowly to face the window. "You and me?"

"In my car with the top down," he said slowly as if gauging how much of a treat she'd find it.

Wow, she'd love to drive in that sexy convertible sports car of his. And she loved the beach.

She *was* supposed to be on vacation.

But to spend the day with Dev? Could she manage that and stay sane?

Taking a deep breath, she decided she liked danger.

Smiling up at him, she drawled, "Sure thing, sugar. Let me clean up and get my suit!"

He laughed. "You almost sound like a Southern belle putting on that accent," he said.

Stricken, Abby tried to hold onto her smile. How could she forget to disguise her voice! Using what he thought was her normal New York accent, she told him she'd meet him at the car.

She almost ran to her apartment, knowing the butterflies in her stomach were the result of living precariously. She was definitely tempting fate by spending so many hours alone with Dev.

But who could resist an invitation to the beach by a devilishly attractive man? She'd had days of practice guarding her secret. She could do it for another few hours.

What she couldn't do was resist the chance to spend those few hours with him. Since Abby had no way of telling what the future held, she'd grab on to today and enjoy herself.

Fifteen minutes later she closed the door to the apartment and started down the stairs. Dev leaned against the garage wall at the foot of the steps, arms crossed, as if he had all the time in the world. His khaki pants ended with bare feet slipped into Docksides. His shirt was a pale green pullover, enhancing his tan, the dark depth of his hair.

But the muscles that showed beneath the shirt drew her attention. He'd be the perfect model for the hospital's Anatomy 101 course--except no nurse in training would give a fig for the name of the muscles, they'd just want to watch him.

Tightening her hands into fists, Abby vowed to keep the afternoon carefree and casual. No giving in to temptation to touch that warm tanned skin to feel the heat. No skimming her fingertips over the muscles, to test the strength beneath.

"I'm ready." She almost groaned at her breathless tone.

He nodded and smiled at her as he pushed away from the wall and reached for her tote. She'd stuffed a towel inside. She wore her suit beneath her shorts and knew she could just pull on her clothes over it once she'd dried from swimming.

"This all?"

"Has my wallet inside, a towel and sunscreen. Do I need anything else?"

"You tell me, Abby Brown." He brushed his lips across hers lightly and watched as if waiting for a reaction.

Abby's heart skipped a beat then raced. She leaned closer, smiling up into his eyes. Slowly she licked her lips, placed one hand on his shoulder, took a deep breath that expanded her chest. Giddy with the knowledge that he'd noticed, she made her voice as sexy as possible when she said,

"Can I drive?"

Chapter Five

Dev roared with laughter. "I thought you were coming on to me."

Abby grinned. "So, can I?"

He raised her chin with the edge of his hand and lowered his face close to hers. Two could play this game. Slowly he perused her, noting the hint of color in her cheeks, the way her blue eyes seemed to shine from within, the wispy blond hair blowing back in the gentle breeze. Then he looked at her mouth, and remembered their kiss by the pool.

"No one drives that baby but me."

She shivered and stepped back, color rising. Satisfied he'd given as good as she'd dished out, he almost smiled as she hurried to the passenger side. For a moment he'd thought she--

Better let that go. He was not looking for any kind of entanglement. A fun afternoon at the beach. That was all.

"It was worth a try," she said when he opened the door for her.

In only seconds, the top was down and the engine on. Buckling her seat belt, Abby leaned back, prepared to enjoy herself. The wind in her hair moments later felt wonderful, blowing away the doubts about what she was trying to do.

When she returned later, she'd have to call her sisters. She'd tell Caroline she was enjoying her vacation. But when she reached Michelle, she'd find out if Josh had discovered anything else about the men they were researching.

For now, however, she gave herself up to the beauty of the day and the excitement of spending it with Dev.

"How close is the beach to Houston?" she asked.

"We'll drive to Galveston. That's about a hour, depending on traffic. I had Thelma pack a lunch for us. Want to listen to the radio? Since you worked in New Orleans, I bet you like jazz."

She nodded.

Dev tuned in an all-jazz station. With the sound of the wind whipping by their ears and the other cars on the highway, conversation was difficult. Abby didn't even try.

When they reached Galveston, Dev drove confidently through town, obviously knowing his way around. Soon he pulled into the driveway of a large home overlooking the Gulf.

"Is this your place?" Abby asked, sitting up. The house was lovely, built of natural cedar with lots of glass on the water side.

"No, it belongs to a friend of my mother's. Since the family lives in Dallas most of the year, we check up on the place for them every so often. The seashore here is quiet, there won't be many people around."

The beach was lovely, Abby thought, as she walked beside Dev a few minutes later on the pristine white sand.

Wide and clean, it seemed to go on forever. Here and there family groups enjoyed the water. Little children built sand castles in the damp sand. Mothers sat beneath umbrellas watching and reading. The crushing crowds sometimes found at public beaches were missing.

"This is wonderful," Abby said, dropping down beside Dev after he spread a blanket and placed the picnic basket on one corner.

"Want to swim first and then eat?"

"Sure." She slipped out of her shorts, pulled her shirt over her head. Looking at Dev, she felt suddenly shy though her one-piece teal blue bathing suit was not daring.

His expression showed pure male interest. Feeling deliciously feminine, she dropped her shirt and turned for the water, conscious of his gaze touching every inch of her. She wanted to return that perusal, but couldn't bring herself to do it.

Splashing into the warm water, she ducked beneath a shallow wave and struck out swimming hard. In no time Dev was right beside her. She should have expected it after seeing all those swimming trophies in his bedroom.

When she was pleasantly tired, she turned over to float. The sky was a cloudless blue, deep and endless. The water felt cool enough to be refreshing, yet warm enough to enjoy without getting chilled.

Dev stopped swimming when she did, lazily treading water beside her as he studied the shoreline, the houses in the background.

"This is nice," Abby said, coming upright and paddling.

"Every summer Houston becomes hot and humid, so coming to the Gulf seems necessary to survival. When I was a kid, I grew up here. Once mom married Sam we used to come and stay with the Stanyons. My dad likes the Gulf--he used to work on some of the rigs off the coast."

Abby went still. Her father had also worked the rigs in the Gulf. Hadn't Edith Strong told Josh and Michelle that he'd worked on the ones near the mouth of the Mississippi River?

"Where?" she asked casually, her heart beating faster.

"Near Brownsville. Ever seen an oil rig?"

"Only pictures."

"Once every five years they gave tours to the families of the men who work on them. I remember going right after Samuel married my mother. It wasn't long after that when he moved up in the company and began buying shares until he eventually obtained controlling interest."

"Your father owns the oil company?" Abby said in shock.

She knew from his lavish home that the Texas contender for the Talmadge girls' father had money, but she hadn't realized how much.

"It's only a regional oil company, not British Petroleum," Dev said, his eyes studying her.

Abby nodded in a daze and began to swim back to the beach. No wonder Dev was wary on his father's behalf. With that much money behind him, he was probably used to people trying to get something for nothing.

When Abby waded out of the water, she debated the

advisability of contacting Josh and reassessing her plan. He'd mentioned nothing about Samuel Williams owning controlling interest in an oil company. Surely he knew. Why let her come into this without that information?

Her plan had seemed so easy when she'd proposed it. Now that she'd met Dev and learned more about his stepfather, she wasn't so sure. Would the man, even if he was her father, suspect she had only sought to find him because of money?

Would Dev?

Trying to shake an odd premonition, Abby sat on the blanket and opened the picnic basket. She'd have to think this through, but later, when she was alone. Right now she had to make sure Dev suspected nothing.

"Wow, Thelma outdid herself. This is a picnic lunch?" she asked as she began to unpack the basket. To her surprise, there were real china plates. She opened some of the containers, finding thin slices of ham and roast beef, mustard, fresh croissants, cold vegetables with a tangy sauce for dipping. For dessert, sugar-sprinkled strawberries.

"What a feast!"

Dev lay down on his side, propped up on his elbow watching Abby select from each container, filling their plates. Her enthusiasm was contagious. He reached out for his dark glasses and pulled them on. Watching her reminded him of days gone by. When he'd been a teenager and everything had been easy and fun.

As an adult, especially lately, he viewed things more cynically. What other woman of his acquaintance would be so delighted with the simple fare Thelma had prepared on such short notice?

Briefly his thoughts flashed to his onetime fiancée, Elizabeth. She had shown only disdain for picnics. Her preference had always been for high-priced restaurants where she could be seen. One of her dresses probably cost more than everything he'd seen Abby wear and then some.

He frowned. He didn't want to think about Elizabeth, or what a fool he'd made of himself over her.

"Don't you like this?" Abby said, offering one of the laden plates.

"Yeah." Dev sat up and reached for the plate.

"So why the frown?"

"Just thinking of someone else."

"Oh? A girlfriend? Probably wishing she was here instead of me."

He looked at her sharply. She didn't seem put out by the thought. And for some reason, that irritated him.

"I don't wish she was here. Elizabeth was nothing but trouble. And nothing like you."

He bit down savagely on the croissant, ignoring the way it almost melted on his tongue.

"How are we different?" Abby began eating, obviously delighting in everything about the outing, from the beach, to the water, to the picnic lunch.

"For one thing, she never showed any of the enthusiasm that you do. Hasn't the novelty of things worn a bit thin?" he asked sarcastically.

"Nope. I think this place is enchanting. I'm having a

great time despite your surly mood. If you don't want to think of Elizabeth, why do it?"

"It pays to remember life's mistakes so they aren't repeated."

"And what life lesson did she teach?"

"Never get involved with anyone whose bank account isn't at least equal to my father's!"

He looked away from her stunned expression. Time she knew the facts of life. He was attracted to her. He enjoyed spending time with her. But that was as far as he was willing to go. It had nothing to do with lord of the manor and an employee, but more with the knowledge that without an equal bank balance, he'd never know for sure a woman wanted him for himself and not his money.

"Define get involved," she said, scooting around on the sand.

He glanced back. She'd put down her plate and was watching him steadily from grave blue eyes.

"Get serious about a woman."

"That sure limits the gene pool." She picked up a sliver of ham and popped it into her mouth.

"What do you mean?"

"If your father owns an oil company, he's probably obscenely rich. Which means there aren't going to be a lot of women your age sitting around on an equal pile of money. And the chances of meeting those who do are slim, therefore your choice is going to be very limited."

Dev watched her finish her roll and wipe the plate with a

napkin. When she looked at him it was with a considerable effort that he didn't question her further.

"I'm going for a walk," she said, pulling on her own dark glasses and standing to head down the beach.

Déjà vu. Hadn't she walked away from their lunch yesterday?

He rose in one smooth movement and joined her by the water's edge.

"You didn't finish your lunch. Thelma will be unhappy if you don't eat the strawberries," he said.

"I'll snack on the ride home," she said, her head held high. "You go eat your share now if you want."

"I'll walk with you," he said, matching his stride with hers.

"Don't bother. Someone might suspect you're becoming involved and I got that message loud and clear."

He detected the hurt underlying her voice.

For some reason he wanted to purge it. True, he had been warning her off, but he hadn't meant to hurt her feelings. They'd spent a few hours together over the last few days. That was all.

Except for those kisses.

But that kind of thing meant nothing. It was kindest to let her know up front he wasn't in any matrimonial stakes.

Not that she had shown a lot of interest so far in this relationship.

Relationship?

No, two people spending a few hours at the beach did *not* constitute a relationship.

"You'll get sunburned," he said as he glanced at her bare shoulders. Her skin was fair, lightly tanned, but the sun, sand and water were a brutal combination. He didn't want her to burn.

He didn't want anything to hurt her, he realized. Including himself. Her sunny disposition was a refreshing experience. He hoped nothing would ever happen to change that for Abby.

She reversed directions and walked quickly back to the blanket. Dev stood watching her. Would she put on sunscreen and head out in the opposite direction to avoid him?

She snatched up her shirt and the bottle of sunscreen and stomped back toward him. Dev was conscious of an easing of his muscles. She was going to continue their walk, even after he'd practically insulted her.

"If you don't mind, would you put some on my back?" she asked frostily, holding out the bottle of lotion.

"If you'll return the favor."

She nodded once and turned around.

Dev opened the cap, poured some of the warm lotion in his palm. Amazing, he thought, in twenty-six years of living, I've never done this before. Slowly he reached out and touched her. Her skin was hot beneath his fingertips, silky soft and smooth. He spread the cream across her back, lingering as he registered the rigid tenseness of her muscles, the delicate bones of her neck and spine. Long after the lotion disappeared, he continued to caress her.

He wanted to turn her around and enfold her in his

arms. See if they could share another kiss as hot as the one by the pool. See if--

"Aren't you finished yet?" She stepped aside and turned back, throwing her shirt over her shoulders. Refusing to meet his eyes, she held out the hand for the sunscreen. "Turn around and I'll do you."

Dev presented his back, gazing over the cool water, wondering if he should just plunge in before he embarrassed both of them with his body's reaction to her touch. Her palms felt firm and competent as she slathered lotion across his back. Closing his eyes for a second, Dev imagined her reaching around to rub some of that lotion on his chest. He could turn in the circle of her arms, and let her coat every inch of exposed skin. The feel of her hands fostered images that he hadn't had in a long time.

Lightly slapping his back, Abby said, "You're done."

He turned slightly, to watch her spread the lotion over her long legs, wishing she'd asked him to do that too. Again images flooded his mind, of his hands rubbing over her legs, and then moving up, over her hips to caress her breasts and then holding her for a deep kiss.

Had the sun fried his brains? He wasn't interested in getting involved. He'd made sure she got that message.

Hadn't he been paying attention himself?

Abby started to walk. Dev debated accompanying her. He'd laid out the ground rules, so there'd be no harm in enjoying the afternoon together.

When he joined her, she glanced at him, and he wished she hadn't put on her dark glasses. Her face was expressionless. What was she thinking?

"Tell me about going to the beach as a child. Did you build sand castles? Practice swimming? Were you ever here during a hurricane?" she asked as they strolled along. The water brushed across their feet, receded.

"You seem to have a curious fixation on hearing about my past," Dev said lightly, wondering why all their conversations seemed to start there.

"It's because I didn't have parents, so I like listening to someone who did. Don't tell me if you don't want."

"I don't mind. But I suspect you already know more about my past than some close friends I've had for years. By the time my mother married Samuel, I was too old to build sand castles. So I didn't come often with him. More with my friends."

"Ha, no one's too old. You just thought you were because you were probably some bratty teenager who thought he was hot stuff."

"Well, that cuts me down to size."

"As if anything could. So if you didn't make sand castles, what did you do?"

"Swimming. Some underwater stuff. The Stanyons have a speedboat over at the marina, so we'd go water-skiing or just take off for the fun of it."

"What does your father look like?" she asked.

"Why?"

"I'm, um, trying to envision the two of you in a boat and can't picture him."

"He's tall. Had thick brown hair when he married Mom, now it's getting gray, but is still thick. His skin is dark--from spending so much time in the sun on the oil rigs, I guess." Dev looked at her. She constantly surprised him. "So now you can picture him and me on a boat?"

She shrugged. "What's your mom like?"

"She's not very tall. She works at keeping gray from her hair. It's sort of a light brown. She still has a nice figure. And is very active, always working for some charity event or the other. Sam's been good for her. She had a hard time with my real dad."

"It's nice, I guess, that they both found happiness the second time around."

"It's not Dad's second marriage," Dev said shortly. "You asked that once and I told you he hadn't been married before. Why do you think he was?"

"I don't. I don't know anything about him. I meant it was nice that they both found happiness and it's your mother's second time."

She spun around and headed for the blanket. "It's getting late. I need to get back. There are things I need to do."

She picked up the pace.

"What's so important on a Sunday afternoon that you have to cut this short to get back for?" he asked, keeping stride with her every step.

"Just things."

When Abby reached the blanket, she pulled on her shorts, buttoned her shirt. "Besides, I don't want to take up all your day, you might suspect some misguided attempt on my part to get involved with you."

Dev shook his head. "You wouldn't even be in the running."

Annoyed afresh at how much his words stung, Abby hastily repacked the lunch things, and walked up toward the vacation house and the car in the driveway. There had already been a strong reason to stay away from Dev. He'd just given her another.

Abby was silent on the ride home. She wondered if there was any way to prove the Houston Sam Williams was her father without having to wait for him to return. Dev hadn't said a word to her once they'd reached the car. She hoped he wasn't rehashing their conversation. Was he beginning to suspect? She thought about the past. Once her mother had died, there was no reason for her father not to remarry. Only--the thought just occurred. How had he known he was free?

Something to ask Josh about.

And stay clear of Dev. With the tenacity he'd shown thus far, once he had a glimmer of the real situation, she wouldn't stand a chance to keep the truth from him. And she still had nearly a week to go! Another six days before she could talk to the man she'd come to see.

Another six days of seeing Dev?

She let her gaze drift over to him. Involuntarily she recalled the feel of his warm skin beneath her hands when she spread the sunscreen. Tightening her fingers into a fist, she tried to ignore the clamoring of her senses to touch again.

In seeking information about the father, she was learning

about the son. She wanted to learn even more. Yet, why? There was no future for them. She only had a couple of weeks left of her vacation. Hopefully she'd discover if Samuel Williams was her father in time to enjoy a bit of her vacation time.

Yet in any case, when her time was up, she had to return to New Orleans, to her new job in the Trauma Unit at the hospital return to her normal life.

New Orleans seemed a long way from Houston.

When Dev pulled into the long driveway, he drove straight to the garage. He shut off the engine and leaned back, looking at Abby.

"Thanks for a nice afternoon," she said.

He laughed, shaking his head. "Ever polite. Your grandmother would be proud."

"I doubt it," she mumbled, gathering her tote and preparing to get out of the car. It was more likely her grandmother'd be spinning in her grave to know Abby was impersonating a gardener!

"Have dinner with me."

"What?"

She looked at him in surprise. After the silent treatment all the way home, after his insistence he was not looking for any involvement, the last thing she expected was an invitation to spend more time with him.

"I don't think so." She opened the door and stepped out. Closing it, she let her hand pat the car one last time. Riding in a convertible had been fun. "See ya." Before she could change her mind, she ran lightly up the stairs to her apartment.

The man was driving her nuts. Coming on to her with one hand, and then slapping her away with the other. Sighing, she pushed away from the door. She'd take a quick shower, fix some soup for dinner and call her sisters.

Michelle wanted to know all about Abby's investigation. Josh was home so Abby was able to ask him about this Sam's marriage.

"If he's our dad, how did he know he was free? I can't see grandmother writing him and letting him know. I'm sure she had no idea where he went after she drove him away."

"Good question. One that might show he's not the one. The other two are not married. We know the New Jersey man isn't your father. There's still the one in California."

She didn't tell him about her involvement with the stepson. She was ending that anyway, so didn't see the need.

When she talked with Caroline, she raved about being at the beach and picnics and late night swims, just not giving all the details. Her sister was doing well and chafing a bit at the coddling she was getting from the family and the recommendations to rest.

Abby laughed and told her to enjoy it. Once the baby was born, sleep deprivation would become a reality.

Monday morning Abby was resigned to either giving up her quest or playing the role of gardener for another few days. She decided to avoid any serious changes to the estate gardens but to give the appearance from a distance of working. She hoped Mrs. Mitton and Thelma hadn't a clue about what was supposed to go on in the yard.

"I'll treat it as in medicine--first do no harm," she

mumbled as she walked around one of the flowerbeds. Though when she glanced around the entire yard her courage almost failed. Even an outsider could see some neglect. Trimming the dead blossoms from the stalks was only a first step. If the plants looked odd or lopsided, she cut the stalks nearer the ground. If she totally ruined something, she'd just have to replace it.

Expecting to be left alone during the week, Abby was surprised at the warm invitation to join them for meals that she received from Mrs. Mitton and Thelma. They insisted she eat lunch and dinner with them, regaling her with tales of places they'd worked. They fussed over her, tempting her with delicacies that Thelma loved to bake. Abby enjoyed herself more than she'd expected.

Dev continued to work long hours. Twice during the week, Abby was already in bed when she heard his car. The other nights, it had taken all her resolve to stay behind closed doors when he arrived home. Definitely no more midnight swims.

After the first dinner, Abby realized she had a gold mine of information ready to be tapped in the two long-time employees. When she had casually asked how long they'd worked for the Williams', she'd been delighted to learn both had been with them for a number of years.

"Nicest folks around. I remember when Dev was a young teenager, he couldn't get enough of my cookies," Thelma said, smiling broadly. "Even now, he always swings by the kitchen when he visits to see if I made a fresh batch."

"Well, I remember how much trouble it was to get him

to put his clothes in the hamper," Mrs. Mitton countered, but the twinkle in her eye left Abby with the feeling the housekeeper hadn't minded a bit. The man was definitely spoiled by the females in his life.

Abby giggled. Hard to believe the rugged businessman was once a typical teenager. Wouldn't he be frustrated to hear that being shared!

"Tell me more. Does Mr. Williams share Dev's love of cookies?"

"He does have a sweet tooth. But he prefers cakes. Mrs. Williams, now, she loves fresh salads and vegetables. Thin as a rail, I say, but she doesn't eat the desserts like her men."

It occurred to Abby as she listened to the stories the women told that she was learning a lot about Dev. None of which would matter if this Samuel Williams didn't turn out to be her father. Nevertheless, she learned more and more, and continued to ply the women with questions.

Thursday evening, Abby showered and donned a pair of light-blue shorts and a short matching crop top. It had been hot and humid all day and she was glad it was drawing to an end. After the rest of the staff retired, she planned to sneak back to the pool and indulge herself in another midnight swim despite her vow to the contrary.

She hoped Dev came home early enough to be asleep by the time she made her clandestine swim.

She slipped on sandals and headed for the main house, hoping Thelma had prepared another one of her salads. It was too hot to eat a heavy meal.

Stepping inside, she noticed immediately that the big kitchen table had only two places set.

"Is Mrs. Mitton not eating with us tonight?" she asked. The air-conditioned room felt heavenly against her heated skin.

Thelma looked up and smiled. "There you are. I set your place on the patio tonight."

"With mine," Dev said, from the doorway between the kitchen and the dining room.

Abby swung around, surprised to see him. "Hi. I didn't know you were here." Had she missed seeing his car in the driveway?

Her heart rate increased slightly and she felt a flush of warmth that the air conditioner couldn't cool at the sight of him. She hadn't seen him since Sunday afternoon. She refused to admit she'd missed him!

She looked at Thelma. "I thought I'd eat in here with you and Mrs. Mitton."

"Oh, go on with you. Dev'd like company for dinner, someone his own age. I've set the table in the shade on the patio. It's cooling off. You two young people have more to discuss than listening to stories Mrs. Mitton and I have to tell."

Dev folded his arms across his chest and leaned casually against the jamb, but Abby wasn't fooled. He was as alert as ever. As he glanced from Thelma to her, she could almost see the speculation rising. Hoping to forestall any questions on his part about what stories she'd been told, she plunged into speech.

"I don't think I should be eating with him. I like eating in here with y'all."

"She thinks of me as lord of the manor," Dev said. His tone was light, his gaze never leaving Abby's.

Thelma laughed. "That'll be the day that a Texan puts on airs. Go on with you, I'll bring out dinner in a bit. There's already a pitcher of iced tea and some rolls on the table." Making a shooing motion, she urged them from the kitchen.

"I can get something on my own," Abby murmured as she reluctantly followed Dev through to the patio.

"And spoil Thelma's matchmaking scheme?"

Her gaze flew to his. "You're not serious?"

Dev encircled her neck with one hand, pulling her close enough that she could feel the heat from his body envelope her. Lowering his head, he rested his forehead on hers, his eyes looking deep into Abby's.

"Oh, yes, Abby Brown. I'm serious. We like each other-- that's the whole problem."

Swallowing hard, she blinked, mesmerized by the desire evident in his eyes.

"But you said you weren't going to become involved with someone like me."

He didn't say a word, merely covered her mouth with his and kissed her.

The world spun and Abby grabbed on to keep from spinning with it. Before she realized it, her arms encircled his neck, and she returned his kiss, reveling in the sensations that swept through her. His tongue sought entry and she parted her lips to enjoy the new sweep of impressions that clamored for expression.

A sound from the house alerted them, and Dev quickly

released her and stepped away. In only a second, Thelma bustled out, carrying a heavily laden tray.

"We'll continue this discussion later," Dev said.

Some discussion, Abby thought, as she moved in a daze to take one of the chairs. Her heart beat rapidly in her chest, her skin felt even hotter than before, and there was definitely something wrong with her breathing.

What was there to discuss? She was afraid she was falling for the man, and he had already firmly posted No Trespassing signs!

Chapter Six

"Hard week?" he asked when Thelma left.

"No. How about you?" Abby tried to smother her guilty feelings. Between the gardening book and YouTube, she had enough information to feel confident in the minimal work she was doing. At least she didn't think she was ruining any plants. The yard was more than she could handle as anyone would see if they looked closely. But she only needed a couple of more days.

She served the salads Thelma had made--a German potato salad and a tasty tuna salad. She sipped her tea and then began to eat, conscious of Dev sitting only a few feet from her. She wanted to look at him, but was too afraid of what her eyes might reveal.

"My week wasn't hard as much as hectic and long. I'll be glad when Dad's back at the helm. Between his vice president, secretary and me we're able to keep going. But he's really missed," Dev said as he began to eat.

"Is he well enough to return right away?"

"Not sure. But he'll be able to come in for a few hours every day I hope."

"I'd think you'd love the chance to run the company," she said. She suspected he'd be good at it.

"I'm not running it. As I said there are three of us working together. It's challenging and exciting. And Dad plans for me to take over when he retires. But that's years away. He's only in his fifties. I have a lot to learn before I'm ready to take complete charge."

"So you're really doing two jobs."

He nodded.

"What's involved in running an oil company?" Maybe she could get him talking, and avoid any awkward questions.

"No you don't. I've noticed every time we're together, you ask questions. Tonight it's your turn to give me some answers."

Abby went still. "What answers?"

She met his gaze, hoping she hid the trepidation his words brought.

"Start with telling me how you ended up specializing in gardening. Or how does the climate and the soil here differ from what you were used to dealing with in Louisiana and New York. Or, how you feel about becoming an aunt."

Smiling spontaneously at the last, she said, "I love the thought of becoming an aunt again. You know that Caroline was pregnant a long time ago and miscarried. This is her second attempt and we're all tiptoeing around her to make sure nothing gets her upset. Not that stress was identified as the cause last time, but we're taking no chances."

"Becoming an aunt again? You're already an aunt?"

"By marriage. My sister Michelle married a man who has a four-year-old daughter. We hit it off instantly. She's adorable."

"You like kids?"

"I'm not around any on a regular basis. But Penny's precious. And I expect to be asked to baby-sit a lot when Caroline's baby arrives."

"That's why you moved here, right? To be near your sister."

Abby held her breath. That had been the cover story. Slowly she nodded. "I want to be near Caroline and watch her baby grow, to be a part of his or her life from the beginning." Stick to the truth as much as possible, she thought.

Dev finished his meal and pushed the plate aside, settling back in his chair. "I'm surprised you aren't married."

"Good grief, I'm just starting out. It's too soon to get married."

"Most women on the far side of twenty-five think time's running out."

Oops, she'd forgotten she was supposed to be older.

"You're not married. And you're on that far side."

He nodded, his expression closing. "I almost married once."

"What happened?" She'd been curious since he mentioned Elizabeth in Galveston.

"It's ancient history now."

"But the reason you want no involvements with women, right?" she guessed shrewdly.

"Right. If you're finished, we could move to the pool deck. The chairs there are more comfortable."

Abby recognized a closed subject when she heard it. But

her curiosity rose another notch. What had happened to make him so cynical about women? Obviously it had to do with his former fiancée, but what specifically?

If she was at all prudent, she'd make some excuse and head for her apartment. Dinner was over, the ordeal safely survived.

But she'd missed him during the week. She could be on guard, watch every word, and take the chance to spend a little more time with him. It was already Thursday. If all went according to plan, by Saturday she'd know the truth about Samuel Williams and be on her way back to New Orleans.

What could one more evening with Dev hurt?

He pulled two lounge chairs into the shade, facing the pool. He eased down on one and leaned back. Gingerly, Abby slipped into the chair next to his. It was still hot, but not unbearably so in the shade. And once the sun went down, it'd become cooler.

The pool looked inviting. Dare she hope he might want to go swimming later?

"What kinds of books do you read?" he asked, once she was settled. "What movies do you like? I know you like jazz, do you like other kinds of music?"

"Bluegrass," she said. "We used to hear it on the riverboats as they made their way upriver when they'd pass Tal--" Stopping suddenly she realized she'd almost given Talmadge Hall as her home. It wouldn't take him two seconds to make the connection to the Miss Talmadge who'd tried to reach his father.

Besides, she was supposed to be from New York.

"Pass where?"

"Uh, Beauregard Point, just outside New Orleans. What kind of music do *you* like?"

"I thought you were from New York," he said slowly.

Yikes! "Um, I am. But we came to visit a cousin who lived in New Orleans. That's why I went there when I was starting out. Always liked it. Anyway, that was ages ago. What's your favorite music?"

She needed to get off the topic of her life. Maybe Josh could think quickly when on an undercover assignment, but she found it full of unexpected traps.

"Some rock and of course country and western. You can't live in Texas and not like country-western music."

Abby smiled.

"Tell me your favorite memory as a child," Dev said.

"My favorite memory? Why?"

"I've shared escapades of my youth with you," he said easily. "Turnabout's fair play."

"Careful, Mr. Hamilton, you sound almost interested."

"And is that a crime?"

"Only if it leads to involvement." Abby knew she skated near the edge, but she couldn't help it.

"Which won't happen. Tell me something, Abby."

"Okay. Let's see. How about the time Bobby Benton and I made a tree fort and played cowboys and Indians for days!"

"How old were you?"

"Twelve." Just before her grandmother began harping on her becoming a lady suitable enough to deserve the Talmadge name.

She launched into the story, embellishing for effect, recalling the sense of freedom she'd felt as they made the fort just the way they wanted, trying to make the scene come alive for Dev. When she finished, she looked over and blinked.

The man had fallen asleep.

Torn between amusement and a sudden feeling of protectiveness, she watched him. His eyelashes made a dark crescent against his tanned skin. Even in sleep, his appeal held. She knew he was tired. And from what he'd said earlier, doing two jobs meant spending long hours at the office every day. She felt an odd sense of contentment that Dev felt comfortable enough around her to completely relax.

Slowly Abby rose and stepped away. She'd let him sleep. He obviously needed that more than companionship.

It was after ten when he knocked on her door. Opening it, Abby grinned up at him. "Next time I'll just stick to the old fairy tales. I understand they're great for putting children to sleep."

"You should have woken me," he said, resting one arm against the door jamb. "Want to go swimming?"

"I thought about it earlier, but now that I've been ensconced in this air-conditioned apartment for a few hours, I don't think so. In fact, I was getting ready to go to bed."

He hesitated a moment, then shrugged, straightening away from the door, looking over the grounds.

"Tomorrow night I have to attend a party one of our customers is giving. It'll be in a hotel downtown. Would you come with me?" He turned back and looked her full in the face.

"Tomorrow night? Why Dev, honey, this is so sudden." Batting her eyelashes, she did her best rendition of a Southern belle.

"Flirting can get you in trouble," he said, running a finger down her cheek.

Abby shivered, feeling his touch to her toes.

Just how much trouble?

"It's not much notice," she said, stalling, amazed to discover how strongly she wanted to go.

"I was planning to attend alone, but thought you might like to go. Make up for my falling asleep on your favorite memory."

"Not necessary. Besides, I work for you."

"For my parents. You sure have a hang-up about that. What if you were a gardener for the next-door neighbors, would you still feel the same about seeing me?"

"Maybe not." But that would never happen. Unless another Samuel Williams moved in next door, she thought whimsically.

"I'll pick you up at seven. It's dressy."

"Then I can truthfully say I don't have anything to wear."

"When are your clothes coming? I thought she said they'd arrived."

"Nothing I own is suitable for a fancy dress dinner. I guess I could quit a bit early tomorrow and see about buying a new dress. I'll make up the time on Saturday."

"I don't think a couple of hours off would hurt anything. See you tomorrow."

For a moment Abby thought he'd kiss her, but he just looked at her for a long moment, then left.

"Another major mistake. What does a twenty-two year old nurse have in common with people in the oil industry who will be at that thing tomorrow night?" she asked herself as she shut the door.

"Doesn't matter, I'll be with Dev. And that's enough!" she answered herself, smiling dreamily.

Promptly at seven the next evening, Dev knocked on her door. Abby had spent the afternoon finding just the right dress. It was a pale blue, with spaghetti straps, a fitted bodice and a swirling skirt. Short and sassy, it fit like a dream. Peering into the mirror, she was pleased to notice the dress made her eyes seem even brighter. Her hair had picked up highlights from her hours in the sun and was glossy and shining.

Maybe she should consider taking up gardening as a hobby. Not that she had a garden at her apartment. But there was always Caroline's house and Michelle's and both had large yards. It'd be a shame to waste all the knowledge she was gaining.

"Wow," Abby said when she opened the door. Dev looked fantastic! He wore a black dinner jacket, with a pristine white pleated shirt. Tall, dark and handsome sprang to mind. Followed immediately by sexy as sin.

"I can see we won't be discussing much business at this event. Once everyone sees you, they'll be otherwise occupied," he returned.

She smiled at the compliment. "The dress is all right?"

"More than all right. It's perfect. You look beautiful."

Warmed by his compliment, by the look in his eyes, she knew she'd enjoy the evening--as long as she kept her wits about her and revealed nothing.

"Since you bought the dress especially for this event, maybe I should reimburse you," Dev said as they began to descend the stairs.

She laughed and shook her head, touched he'd even think to offer.

"Men don't buy women's clothes--unless they're married. Besides, I can always wear this at the hospital Christmas ball--"

Oops. So much for revealing nothing. They hadn't even left yet.

"The hospital?" he asked, opening the passenger door to his car. Tonight the top was up.

"Um, the hospital near where I used to live has a charity event every Christmas. I usually go. To support them and all," she trailed off. Darn it, she was so not used to this subterfuge.

"But that's in New York and you'll be here this Christmas, won't you?"

"I might go there to visit...friends." How could a person working undercover ever keep everything straight, she wondered. "Tell me about the party. I suspect it'll be huge if it's being held at a hotel ballroom."

"Titan Brothers is a major liquid petroleum trucking firm with offices all over the state and Oklahoma. They're trying to convince us to let them be the exclusive shipper for our oil. Every August they throw a big party and invite everyone they know. Jim-Bob Titan is the CEO. His wife, Lily, uses the event as an excuse to buy new clothes, and jewelry, to show off to the world."

"Umm. Do you go every year?"

"Usually. My folks usually attend. Jim-Bob and Dad go back a long way. This will be the first year my parents have missed."

When they arrived at the hotel, Abby was reminded of the glittering charity events she attended with her grandmother in Baton Rouge. Because of her grandmother's training, she was easily able to converse confidently, knowing when to be serious, and when to be amusing. Flirting a little with the older men and keeping a distance from the younger, she enjoyed herself.

The meal was delicious. But the dancing was the best part.

Being held in Dev's arms, twirling around the floor, watching other couples swaying to the music was heavenly.

"I thought you'd do the Texas Two-Step," she murmured as another waltz began.

Dev smiled at her. "Not at such a fancy event. But we can hunt up a place another night and give it a whirl if you like."

Abby felt her bones melt at the sight of his smile. Glad she had his shoulder and hand to hold her up, she nodded, looking away before she did something silly like move closer and give him an indication about how she felt.

Not that she wanted to examine those feelings closely.

The night was young, and she didn't want introspection to interfere with having a good time.

They nibbled from the sumptuous buffet tables, sipped wine from the lavish bar. Names swirled around and around as she tried to remember everyone Dev introduced to her.

There were odd speculative glances thrown her way. After one, Abby looked down at her dress, down to her shoes.

"Is there something wrong with me?" she asked, looking back at Dev.

"What do you mean?"

"People keep giving us odd looks. Did I spill something on my dress?"

He scanned her from head to toe. "There's nothing on your dress."

"Then why--"

He shrugged, sipping the wine. "Probably because I haven't brought a date in years."

"Oh." Oddly pleased, she suddenly wondered why. It was just a casual date. Nothing to read into it.

"Hello, Dev." A tall man stopped in front of Dev and shook hands.

"Tyler."

"And this is?" Tyler asked as he smiled at Abby.

"Abby Brown," Dev said, offering nothing more.

"Would you care to dance, Abby Brown?" Tyler asked, holding out his hand.

"I came with Dev." She looked at him.

"Dance with him if you want," Dev said carelessly.

Abby hesitated, then smiled and shook her head. "Thanks anyway. I'll just sit this one out with Dev."

Tyler looked nonplussed. "Something going on here I should know about?" he asked.

Dev regarded Abby, his eyes narrowed slightly. "Nothing's going on. But you heard the lady, she doesn't want to dance."

Tyler murmured something polite and moved on.

"What was that about?" Dev asked. "Most women would love to dance with Tyler. Be seen, admired."

Abby blinked. "First of all, I have no interest in Tyler whatever-his-last-name was. I didn't come here to be seen or admired. You invited me. I thought you wanted to spend time with me. I wanted to spend time with you. Why would I want to cut that short by dancing with someone else?"

"Why indeed," Dev said, taken with her explanation.

Taking her glass, he put his and hers on the bar and drew her to the dance floor. Gathering her close, they moved in time to the tempo.

Dev breathed in her fragrance. Since that first day, he'd felt something different about Abby Brown. And trying to figure out what it was occupied more time than it should.

But he wasn't sorry she'd refused Tyler. Puzzled by it, definitely.

Elizabeth would have been off in a shot. She loved to attend events where she could be the belle of the ball, loved to be the center of attention. And pouted if she didn't have her own way.

Tightening his hold on Abby, Dev stopped thinking

about the other woman and concentrated on the one in his arms. She was soft and sweet, with a sensuality that he suspected she didn't recognize. Her scent surrounded them, enhanced by the warmth of her skin. He liked it. It wasn't cloying like some women wore, but light and fragrant.

In fact, he found he liked a lot about Abby Brown.

But that's as far as he was willing to go. He'd been burned once and didn't plan to repeat the experience.

They circled the floor and Dev realized neither of them had spoken a word since beginning the dance. Other women seemed to feel duty-bound to chat incessantly when dancing. With Abby, they both could enjoy the music and each other.

To his surprise, he realized he was enjoying the dance-- and the woman in his arms.

When the song ended, Jim-Bob Titan clapped Dev on the back.

"Hello, boy. Saw you earlier, but with this crush, I couldn't get over to talk to you before now. How're you doing? How's your dad? I heard he's doing better."

"Hello, Jim-Bob. Dad's recovering. He and Mom will be home tomorrow. The ship docked in New Orleans this afternoon. They're flying home in the morning."

"Well, you tell him hey for me and Lily. Now who's this lovely lady with you? Haven't seen you bring a date to this event in years. Not since that skinny gal you were tangled up with."

"This is Abby Brown. Abby, Jim-Bob Titan, our host."

"Nice to meet you, sir."

"Yessirree bob, I like this one, Dev. Got manners and

looks. Glad you came, pretty lady. You having a good time?"

"I surely am, Mr. Titan."

"Jim-Bob, honey. Just Jim-Bob. I've known this boy since he was a youngster. If he gives you any trouble, you come tell old Jim-Bob."

Abby smiled and nodded. "I'll keep that in mind."

"I'm trembling in my shoes," Dev said, his eyes twinkling.

Jim-Bob laughed, clapped him on the shoulder again. "That'll be the day. There hasn't been anyone to do anything with you since you grew up. I know your daddy's proud of you. I heard you've been keeping the company going in his absence. From a customer's point of view, you're doing fine."

Dev nodded. "I appreciate that, Jim-Bob."

"Yessirree bob, your daddy has some big shoes to fill, but you can do it. Won't have to for a few years, though, right?"

"Right. He'll be back to normal in no time."

"See that this pretty lady enjoys herself, you hear me?"

Dev nodded again, shaking hands with the older man.

"Whew," Abby said when Jim-Bob had moved on to greet another guest. "He has a lot of energy, doesn't he? I like him--but I bet his wife has her hands full with him!"

"Lily can handle him. And he dotes on her."

It was late by the time they left even though the revelry continued. Dev enjoyed the quiet ride home, basking in the contentment the evening had brought.

"I had a wonderful time. Thanks for inviting me. Who

was that skinny woman you brought last?" she couldn't resist asking.

"Elizabeth--my ex-fiancée."

"Ah, the one who made you swear off women forever."

"Got it in one," he said as he pulled the car into the driveway and stopped at the base of the apartment stairs. Switching off the engine, he looked at her.

"You know what I think?" Abby said, unfastening her seat belt.

"I suspect you're going to tell me." To his surprise, he was looking forward to hearing what she thought.

She leaned close. "I don't think you've looked into the mirror lately. You've got so much going for you that it would be a pity if you were scared off relationships forever."

Daringly, she kissed him, brushing her lips against his. Then she opened her door and ran up the steps to her apartment. Fumbling for the keys, she had them in the lock by the time he caught up with her.

"Do you call that a good-night kiss?" he asked, drawing her into his arms.

His mouth searched for, then settled on hers. He could feel her respond.

Endless minutes later Dev slowly pulled away. They were both breathing hard.

"You're a dangerous woman, Abby Brown."

"Just think about what I said," she responded, opening her door. "Good night. And thanks again for taking me."

As Dev walked toward the main house, he wished the evening had gone on longer.

The next morning, Abby called Josh.

"What's up?" her brother-in-law asked.

"Nothing yet. But Samuel Williams comes home today."

"Let me know what you discover. Brandon is set to fly to the Coast next Wednesday to interview that Sam Williams. If you find out anything before then, let us know. You might save him the trip."

"I hope I can find out today," she said. Nerves were drawn tight as she thought about finally facing the man who might be her father. "How's Caroline?"

"Doing fine. Want to talk to Michelle?"

"Yes."

The conversation was short, and Abby kept listening for the sound of a car. She hadn't a clue what time to expect Dev's parents, but she wanted to be present to see them when they arrived. Would that be enough? There were no photographs she'd ever seen of her father. What did he look like. Would she recognize him somehow, or father or not would he still be a total stranger?

Hanging up the phone, Abby moved to the window. What would Dev say if it turned out his step-father was her real father after all?

Chapter Seven

Abby deliberately delayed providing the flowers for the rooms in the main house until late Saturday morning. If she timed it right, she'd still be fussing with the arrangements when Dev's parents arrived. Armed with several large vases she'd found in the garden shed and an armful of freshly cut flowers, she entered the kitchen, explaining to Mrs. Mitton and Thelma in passing that she planned to put flowers in each of the downstairs rooms as she breezed through to the main portion of the house.

She found it fun to arrange the flowers, delighting in the visual pleasure of the various shades and hues, savoring their sweet fragrances. Abby did her best to take her time. Stalling as long as she dared, she finally had to give up when Mrs. Mitton peeked into the dining room for the third time.

"I think all the arrangements look lovely," she said, as if puzzled by Abby's delay.

"I want them perfect. First impressions and all," she murmured vaguely, hoping the housekeeper would attribute an anxiousness to please as the reason for her lengthy time. Where were the Williams'? Would they be home soon?

"I'm sure Mrs. Williams will love them. Will you be eating lunch with us?"

"Yes. I'm not going anywhere today." At least not before she met Sam Williams.

Mrs. Mitton didn't move until Abby reluctantly backed away from the final arrangement.

"I guess I'm finished." She gathered the leftover blossoms and cut ends, wrapping them in the damp newspaper she'd used to keep the flowers fresh while she was arranging them.

Walking toward the gardening shed a few minutes later, Abby looked around the yard hoping inspiration would strike. There had to be something she could do to be on hand when Dev's parents arrived without being awkwardly obvious.

Staring at the different gardening implements, she came up with an idea. She reached for the rake. She'd pretend to work where she could watch the driveway and make sure she didn't miss anything.

It was hot. The sun beat down from a cloudless sky. Slowly she dragged the rake over and over the grass. Had Dev been supposed to meet them at the airport? Unlikely with his small car. They may not even arrive until dinnertime, or later. Was she going to spend all day raking this one spot of lawn?

Fanning her face with her hand, she wondered if she could last all day. Maybe if she moved to the side of the house, she could keep the driveway in view and garner a bit of shade.

When the Williams' did arrive, Abby almost missed them. The limo from the airport pulled quietly right up to the front door. Dashing around the side of the house when she realized what was happening, she stopped in time to see a tall man walk up the shallow steps and disappear through the front door. Mrs. Mitton was already on the stairs greeting the new arrivals, blocking him from Abby's view.

Scarcely looking at the woman who followed him inside, Abby felt numb. She'd glimpsed the man, and still hadn't a clue if he was her father.

"Oh, Abby," Mrs. Mitton said as she turned to speak to the driver. "The Williams are home."

"So I see. Can I help carry anything inside?" Abby asked on the spur of the moment.

"The driver will take in the heavier bags. Maybe you could take this one?"

Dropping the rake, Abby went to take one of the carry-on bags. Mrs. Mitton carried the other.

Entering the house, Abby glanced around. The foyer was empty. She heard the murmur of voices from upstairs. She was on the bottom step when Mrs. Mitton came in beside the driver.

"Oh, just put it down, Abby. I'll get them sorted and take them upstairs later. Run along to the kitchen, Thelma has lunch ready. They would arrive just as we were ready to eat. But Thelma already has started a tray to take upstairs. Mr. Williams is going to lie down. And if I know Mrs. Williams, she's already calling Dev. I told him they'd be here this morning. But he would have to do some more catch-up at the office. Honestly!"

Reluctantly Abby set the case down. With one more

glance up the stairs, she headed for the kitchen. How could she be so close and yet miss them?

As soon as she finished lunch, Abby slipped out. She was too frustrated to make conversation. Her mind was spinning with trying to come up with ways to meet Sam Williams. In retrospect, she should have held off on the flowers. She could have taken the arrangements inside once they had arrived and made sure she included a bouquet for the upstairs sitting room. Maybe she could have glimpsed the man from the open door.

Now she had no excuse for re-entering the house today.

Walking back to the front yard, she picked up the rake, scanning the windows. Wouldn't Sam wish to look out over his estate? He'd been gone several weeks.

No one appeared at any of the windows.

Standing in the shade of the old elm, she studied the house. Which room was the master bedroom? Wasn't it the one on this corner? Dev had shown her the upstairs once, yet she felt turned around. She thought it was this room. She gazed up, wishing she could glimpse inside, just to see what the man looked like.

She thought she'd developed some patience working in medicine. But it seemed to have deserted her. She'd already been in Texas more than two weeks. She didn't want to wait any longer!

There had to be a way to see the man today.

Suddenly--an idea. Five minutes later she carefully leaned the sturdy ladder from the shed against the tree. It easily reached that first solid branch. She could climb out on that limb and almost touch the house--close enough to see inside. Thanks to her escapades with Bobby Benton, she was adept at climbing trees.

"Though I never expected to play Peeping Tom," she murmured, wrestling the ladder into the precise position she wanted.

Awkwardly holding a set of pruning shears for cover in case someone spotted her, she started up the ladder.

"Josh would be proud of my resourcefulness," she mumbled as she balanced herself on the sturdy branch. If anyone caught her she'd say she was pruning.

Inching out, she was glad for her tomboy past. Climbing trees had been a lark when she was younger, but it assumed a different perspective as an adult. If she fell, she could seriously injure herself. But she wouldn't fall. And she only had a few feet more to go--

"What the hell are you doing up there?"

"What?" Abby swayed, lost her balance and frantically reached above her to grab another limb. The shears dropped to the ground. Heart pounding, Abby peered down through the leaves straight into Dev's face.

"You scared me to death! I could have fallen!"

Of all the rotten luck! She'd love to see Dev at any other time. But not now!

"Why are you up there to begin with?"

Frantically she sought an excuse. "I'm cutting back some of the tree--pruning, you know."

"In August?"

Wasn't August as good a month as any other?

124 | Barbara McMahon

From the disbelief in his tone, she suspected it must not be the most auspicious month for pruning.

"Umm, I saw some, uh, diverticulum which is deadly for trees. I wanted to cut that out."

"Show me this diverticulum. If there is any such thing," he said stepping closer to the ladder. "Or are you up there on a spying mission?"

Color flooded her face. She couldn't say a word, only stare at him. How had he guessed?

"The problem is, you wouldn't see anything if I'm down here," he said.

"What?"

"What do you hope to see peering into my room? You saw it the other day, so why do you want to see it from this angle?"

Abby looked at the window so tantalizingly near. The glare on the glass prevented her from seeing inside at all.

"Your room?" she squeaked. "That's your room?"

Dev laughed sardonically. "Nice touch, Abby. As if you didn't know it's my room. Care to show me this deadly disease that threatens the tree?"

Sheer relief made her almost giddy. He thought she was trying to see into *his* room. He didn't know she wanted his father's.

Inching along the limb, embarrassment swept through her. Josh definitely would not be impressed with this escapade. But she could imagine her sisters hooting with laughter. Maybe it was something best left unrelated when she returned home.

"Ummm, actually, now that I'm up here and can see the leaves up close, I think I may have been mistaken."

Slowly she made her way back to the ladder and started down.

Dev startled her when he reached up and took her around the waist, swinging her to the ground.

His smoldering eyes on her, he leaned forward. "What's really going on?"

"What do you mean?"

She met his gaze, hers as impassive as she could make it. If only she didn't feel the heat staining her cheeks. "What are you doing here, anyway? With your parents' return, I thought you'd be in with them," she said, hoping to divert his attention.

"I came to find you so you can meet my mother."

"Taking me home to meet Mother? Isn't this sudden?"

"She's your boss," he said coolly, pulling away. "I thought you'd want to meet her."

She tried to be flippant to ease some of the tension that still filled her. Now into the fray, meeting his mother--and maybe his father?

Dev walked beside Abby wondering what she had been doing in the tree. His windows were closed. She'd seen his room before, why try to peer into it now? That excuse about some tree disease rang false. The tree looked healthy to him.

Her sassy remark about meeting his mother brought back Elizabeth's efforts to ingratiate herself with his parents. She'd been so attentive, hanging on their every word, telling him how much she'd like to be just like his mother.

It was only later that he realized what she'd meant was be as rich as his mother. Money was the most important thing in Elizabeth's life.

Had he made a mistake in Abby? If she thought their date Friday gave her an inside track, he'd have to set her straight. His mother was her new boss, not a prospective in-law.

Scowling, Dev lengthened his stride.

Where had that thought sprung from? He'd spent some time with Abby, that's all. Nothing serious. They'd shared a couple of kisses, a few dances, a trip to the beach and one midnight swim. He certainly wasn't considering anything more involved. If they chose to spend some casual time together, it didn't automatically lead anywhere.

If and when he felt the need to get married, it'd be with someone he knew wasn't in it for the money!

Rounding the corner of the house, he slowed just a bit to let Abby catch up. He wanted to watch her reactions when she met his mother. He could tell a lot by how a person reacted.

Ruth Williams was sitting on the patio beneath one of the large umbrellas that shaded a table. A pitcher of lemonade and several glasses were on the table. She smiled at Dev, warmth and love evident in her gaze. When she looked at Abby, her expression became speculative, but her smile remained warm and welcoming.

"Hello, I'm Ruth Williams."

"How do you do? I'm Abby Brown."

"Do sit down. I know you have Saturdays off, but I

hope you don't mind meeting this afternoon. We'll discuss the garden plans on Monday. I just wanted to meet you today, and thank you for the lovely arrangements throughout the house. What a nice welcome home."

"I'm happy to meet you," Abby said, sitting gingerly on the edge of the chair when Ruth indicated she should join her.

Dev pulled up a chair on the other side of his mother and sat. So far Abby had done nothing to indicate she was trying to ingratiate herself with his mother.

Yet something felt off kilter.

Ruth poured lemonade for each of them, then settled back in her chair. "Tell me something about yourself Abby. You seem young to be a master gardener."

She took a sip of her beverage and gave a polite smile. As she spoke, Dev's attention drifted. He liked looking at Abby. In the shorts she wore, her long legs looked smooth and tanned. He wanted to reach out and run a fingertip along the length of her calf, feel that silky skin.

He wanted more. To thread his fingers through her soft hair. Cradle her head and kiss her--feeling like he'd explode with the sensations touching her always roused.

When there was a lull in the conversation, he spoke lazily, watching Abby.

"Do you think Dad'll be up for dinner?"

"Oh, yes," Ruth replied smiling. "He really didn't want to lie down, I convinced him to do so. I know he's fully recovered, but it was such a scare that I want him to take all precautions. He'll be down for dinner. He's already asked

Thelma for some of her barbecue ribs. There'll be no holding him back from those."

For a moment Dev almost asked Abby to join them. Wouldn't that surprise his mother? She wouldn't think anything about her son dating the "hired help" like Abby protested so often. But he wanted to wait until his mom knew Abby better before springing that on her.

Since Elizabeth, if he even mentioned a woman's name, his mother got a certain hopeful look in her eye.

And a few dates and kisses did not a new daughter-in-law produce.

Not that he thought Abby was interested in that role anyway. She was more likely to argue with him than flatter. More inclined to be difficult than compliant. And a lot more interested in hearing about his childhood than what he was doing now.

Maybe that was some of her charm. So far she had seemed singularly unimpressed by his money or position.

"I've enjoyed meeting you, Abby, but I don't want to take up your weekend," Ruth said. "We'll discuss the plans for the garden on Monday. This is your day off and I'm not a slave driver."

"Seemed like it sometimes when I was a kid," Dev said, still watching Abby.

She seemed to grow more relaxed. But she still sat on the edge of her chair as if ready to dart away.

And she kept glancing at the house.

"I look forward to our working together," Ruth said graciously after frowning at her son.

Dev stood. He recognized a dismissal when he heard one.

"I'll help you carry the ladder back, if you like."

"Ladder?" Ruth asked, looking from one to the other. Abby rose and placed her glass on the table.

"I was examining something in a tree and needed the ladder."

"Suspected diverticulum," Dev added.

Ruth frowned. "What is diverticulum? Sounds like a medical term."

"Apparently a rampant disease that can affect elms, right Abby?" Dev answered.

"Upon closer examination, I found no trace of the disease," she said stiffly.

Next time she'd have to come up with some other kind of disease. She was hitting too close to home. "Your trees look quite healthy."

Abby walked swiftly to the ladder, frustration barely held in check. "I can manage just fine, thank you. I brought it out here, I can take it back."

"I don't mind helping you."

"I don't need your help!"

"Is the heat making you cranky?" he asked. "Or is it me?"

She stopped and glared at him. "Go visit with your mother."

Amusement swept through him. She looked like she could spit nails. He brushed the hair back from her cheek, letting his fingers linger on the soft warmth of her skin. Her cheeks were rosy and her eyes a sparkling blue.

Desire ached deep inside. Giving in to the urge, he leaned over and kissed her. His fingers threaded in her silken hair as he'd wanted, but he didn't draw her into his arms. The kiss was enough. Sweet, delicate, ardent--packing enough wallop that he suddenly craved more.

She pushed away and he let her go.

"A nice dip in the pool would cool you off," he said. It'd cool him off, as well, and he could use it about now.

"No, thanks." She reached for the ladder, but Dev brushed her aside and hefted it on his shoulder. "Lead on, McDuff."

Gathering the pruning shears and rake, Abby stomped away. He followed, enjoying the view of her swaying hips, her long legs. Her back was ramrod straight as if to display her displeasure with him in every tantalizing inch. Instead of putting him off, it only furthered his interest.

Abby Brown was one sexy package.

The shed was stifling. Placing the ladder on its pegs, Dev quickly left, waiting while Abby locked it shut.

"If not a swim, how about a ride?"

"Shouldn't you be with your parents? They just got back."

"They were only gone three weeks. And I'll see them at dinner. Come on, you can show me where your sister lives."

Abby's eyes widened. "They're not home this weekend."

"So we won't stop, just drive by."

"It's too hot to be driving around with the sun beating down on us."

"So I'll put up the top, turn on the air-conditioning."

"Why have a convertible if you don't use it?"

He cupped the nape of her neck and shook her gently. "You are the most contrary woman I know. We'll have the car however you like it."

"I'd need to shower and change," she said slowly.

"Then hurry up."

She hesitated a moment, as if to argue again, then shrugged and headed for her apartment.

Dev watched her walk away, wondering what he thought he was doing spending more time with her.

The anticipation that began to build at the thought of spending the afternoon together warned him he was getting in too deep.

After today, he'd cut back on seeing Abby. Put their relationship into perspective.

Relationship? He rubbed the back of his neck and headed for the house.

Maybe he was in too deep already.

Abby showered in record time. Slipping into a new sun dress, she quickly dried and brushed her hair. Despite her failed attempts to see Sam Williams, the day felt bright and exciting. She was going to spend several hours with Dev! Maybe he'd invite her to dinner and she'd have a chance to meet his father without relying on subterfuge.

She hesitated, brush still raised as she gazed at herself in the mirror. What happened once she met the man? Would she know instantly if he were her father or not? A few judicially placed questions and she'd have an answer. Either way, she had no reason to remain in Texas after she found out the truth.

"All the more reason to make the most of this afternoon," she said, laying the brush down. This could be her final outing with Dev. Refusing to dwell on the distress the notion brought, she reached for her small purse, slipped the strap over her shoulder and headed outside.

Dev waited for her again, as he had the last time, leaning against the garage, one foot resting on the wall. He glanced up at Abby as she ran lightly down the steps. Her heart soared when she saw him. At the same time her sense of preservation kicked in.

Don't be getting too chummy with him, she admonished herself. Futilely. She was already in over her head!

Settled in the car, top up and air conditioning on, she gazed out the window as Dev drove away from the estate, doing her best to ignore the compelling desire to gaze at him.

"Where to?" he asked

"Anywhere," she said.

"We could go to Mercer Arboretum or the Houston Arboretum. Both have exhibits of native Texas plants. Is that something you'd like?"

"Would you?"

He shrugged. "Plants aren't my life, but I thought you might enjoy seeing the local indigenous varieties. Or we could drive through Heights and see samples of Victorian gardens. Or try something totally different and head for the Space Center."

She laughed softly. "You sound like a tour guide."

"At your service, ma'am."

"If it weren't so hot, I'd say let's head for one of the arboretums."

"There'll be plenty of shade."

Touched he chose a spot for her benefit, Abby resolved to enjoy herself. She wasn't highly interested in plants, but he didn't know that. And she did enjoy looking at gardens. Today it was his company she craved more than anything. She would take what he offered, greedily hoarding every memory.

And maybe learn a bit more about Dev Hamilton.

"Where did you go to school?" she asked.

"High school here in Houston, college at the university in Austin." He turned on the station playing soft jazz.

"Did you ever work on the oil rigs like your father?"

"A couple of summers, nothing like he did. He said the experience was good for the business, but beyond that, it didn't contribute to working in an office."

"Did you like it?"

"Yeah, it was hot and hard work, but challenging."

"Yet you find working at the main office challenging, too, don't you?"

"In a different way. Do you find your work challenging?"

Nursing?

"Yes. I'm still so new at it, I know I don't have all the knowledge or experience I need. But I do the best I can and still study."

He glanced at her, frowning slightly. "With several years experience, I'd think you'd feel more confident."

The cover story! "Well, I still think there's lots I don't know."

"There are a lot of men who work as landscape architects, I'm surprised you haven't found one to suit you."

"What does that mean?"

"I'm still curious why you aren't married."

"Maybe I think I'm better off on my own. What's your excuse?"

"I told you--"

"No, Dev, I mean what really happened? Did she cheat on you? Or throw you over for someone else? Whatever it was, you are sure anti-marriage now."

"Not so. My folks have a great marriage. Just as a marriage is supposed to be, open, loving, committed. They have a lot in common, share interests, friends."

"And you didn't have that with your fiancée?"

He turned into the parking lot of the arboretum, pulling into a shady spot and killing the engine. Turning slightly he looked at Abby.

"Elizabeth was perfection. She liked everything I liked, wanted to do everything I wanted to do. The perfect corporate wife--good at working a room at a party, always supportive."

"But?"

He hesitated long enough that Abby wondered if he was going to answer her. Finally he did. "But she was in it for the money. For what my money would buy her. She wanted a glamorous lifestyle and picked me as the man most likely to give it to her. And she worked hard at being the perfect

woman for me. Only--there was no emotion, no feelings, and
certainly no commitment!"

"Oh."

"Oh? Is that all you have to say? Would you treat a man
like that, Abby? Would you lead him on with an agenda of
your own? Pretend he's all you want, when in reality it's what
he can provide that you want?"

"Not all women are like that."

"That's true. But enough are."

"So you'll wait for a woman who can buy and sell your
father before becoming involved."

"Right."

"What if she suspects you are after her money?"

He studied her for a moment. "Interesting thought, isn't
it? Come on."

Abby ached for the younger Dev, who had loved
Elizabeth enough to ask her to marry him before discovering
she didn't love him. He was a proud man, taking pride in his
accomplishments, in his own innate integrity. It must have
hurt a lot.

She wanted to gather him close and soothe away that old
hurt.

And he'd probably laugh until the middle of next week if
she tried.

Taking his hand, she squeezed it a bit. It was the most
she could offer.

Dev laced his fingers through hers, but said nothing as
they walked toward the entrance.

The afternoon was perfect, Abby realized a little while

later. They wandered alone on one of the paths, shaded by the old trees. The planting beds were full of colorful flowers that she hadn't a clue what to call. Neat little signs identified each cluster and she tried to surreptitiously read each one in case Dev asked her to identify any plants. She hoped her luck held.

He seemed relaxed, and she enjoyed the small talk they exchanged. She'd say more, but she was still wary of his remembering the voice of the woman on the phone. It seemed like another lifetime when she had first called him. Yet it was only two weeks.

Amazing. Now she couldn't imagine not knowing Dev.

Not loving him.

Abby froze. Dev took two steps, his arm outstretched with hers, before he realized she'd stopped.

"What's wrong?"

She blinked and looked at him. Her heart beat a furious tempo. She couldn't have fallen in love that fast. And not with Dev Hamilton. Averting her eyes, she tried to summon a smile.

"Nothing's wrong, I just want to study this flower for a minute."

But her eyes couldn't focus on the blue blossom.

She tried to slow her rapid pulse. Tried to think rationally. But the fact wouldn't go away. She was in love with Dev Hamilton.

Falling in love with him was probably the dumbest mistake she'd ever made.

Chapter Eight

Abby wanted to go home. To escape the emotions that threatened to overwhelm her. To gain some solitude in order to think through her amazing discovery.

How could she have let herself fall in love? What was she doing? Dev had made it abundantly clear he had no interest in marriage--and especially not with her.

And the sudden thought of all the years ahead that wouldn't hold Dev in her life dismayed her.

"I need to get back," she said stiffly.

"Are you all right?"

"I think the heat's getting to me." As an excuse it was feeble, but it'd have to do. She needed some space--and time to think.

Not that thinking would change anything. There was no future with Dev. She knew the futility of wishful thinking. Hadn't she been present when a patient wouldn't respond to treatment? Hadn't she railed against fate more than once--to discover it never changed things?

The ride home seemed interminable. Abby silently urged Dev to drive faster. His presence fed her dismay. She yearned to be more than a casual date--to mean something to him, become important in his life.

Dev looked over at her several times, as if to check that she was still there. The air-conditioning in the car cooled her, but she refused to meet his gaze.

"You can use the pool tonight if you like. My parents usually go to bed around eleven, so a midnight swim wouldn't be detected."

"Thanks."

Go swimming again? Remember the night they'd shared the pool? She didn't think that was something she dare do. She had enough memories to make her ache with longing, no sense deliberately adding to her turmoil.

Was there another way?

Of course it'd be hard to show up one day three years younger and with a nursing degree.

Who was she fooling? He had no interest in her beyond a casual date here and there. If there were strong feelings on both sides, they could work things out. But he'd never given a hint he was growing to care for her. To him, she was a novelty. When he looked for a wife, it would be in the echelons of the rich and famous.

Could she win a lottery?

Wait a minute! Did she truly want a man who thought money was so important he wouldn't even look at a woman unless she matched his net worth?

In a heartbeat--if it was Dev, she admitted.

He pulled into the spot where he normally parked and stopped the engine.

"Thank you. I had a nice time."

"Ever the proper response," he murmured, brushing the

back of his fingers along her cheek. "Are you going to be all right?"

"I'll be fine." She opened the door and almost ran to the stairs.

But being alone didn't help, all her thoughts centered on Dev.

Eating a sandwich later for dinner, Abby restlessly roamed around the tiny apartment, feeling alone and abandoned. She tried calling her sisters, but neither answered. Not that they could do much, but she longed to hear their familiar voices, listen to Caroline's advice, or Michelle's calm suggestions.

She needed to get this over with. She felt stretched tight as a drum. Maybe tonight. She'd calmly walk up to Sam Williams and--

Her mind went blank.

No matter what, she couldn't imagine what she'd say. She'd just have to hope something came to mind when she was on the spot.

Walking out into the evening heat, she wandered around the yard, wishing she knew more about taking care of the plants. She looked up when she neared the patio. The aroma of barbecue wafted on the air. Her mouth watered. A sandwich didn't compare with a Texas barbecue.

Screened from the patio by the high hedge that ran along one side, she drew close without anyone seeing her.

Yet she could see them through the leaves. Dev and his parents sat around one of the large tables. Sam had his back to her. She could see him gesturing. A minute later Ruth and Dev burst out laughing.

Abby watched for a long time. She and her sisters had rarely enjoyed eating outside. It was not something their grandmother had approved of. And there had been no laughing or such obvious enjoyment when they'd dined at Talmadge Hall--everything had been much too formal.

Abby found her gaze resting on Dev. He looked relaxed, amused, happy. Obviously his family enjoyed a close bond.

Except with her sisters, she'd never felt such a tie. Which made her feel sad and envious--and even more lonely.

Turning away, she knew she wouldn't approach Sam Williams tonight. She wouldn't be the one to disrupt such a happy evening.

There was always tomorrow.

Abby didn't feel like sleep. She tried to read the gardening book, but threw it aside after a few pages.

Heading for the bedroom, she began to pack her things. There wasn't much, only the few shorts and sun dresses she'd bought since she'd been in Texas. Of course the dress she'd worn to the party couldn't be crushed in a suitcase. Touching it lightly, she smiled wistfully. Another memory to tuck away.

The knock on the door startled her. Knowing instinctively who it was before she opened it, she couldn't control the delight that filled her.

"Hi." He leaned against the jamb, looking down at her with those sexy silvery-gray eyes.

"Hi." Original. Why couldn't she be different, fascinating. Beguiling? Make him so crazy for her he'd overlook everything?

"Want to go swimming?"

No, no, no. The last thing she needed was to put herself anywhere near a half-naked man who already drove her crazy.

"Sure. I'll meet you there in a few minutes. I need to change." Was that voice hers? What happened to no?

"I'll wait." Pushing her gently, he backed her into the apartment and closed the door behind him.

"Are your parents asleep?" A quick glance at the clock showed it was not that late.

"In bed in any event. My mother likes to read before falling asleep and I noticed the light's on in their room. Their bedroom faces the front of the house so they won't hear us in the pool."

"Oh. I'll just be a minute."

Slipping into the silken water a few moments later, Abby threw caution to the wind. One more night couldn't hurt. She couldn't fall any more in love. And to spend a precious few hours with Dev seemed only fair when she would soon be back in New Orleans--all alone.

They swam, then held on to the side of the pool and talked softly. Reluctant to leave the water, almost floating, Abby let her legs entangle with Dev's. Darkness cloaked them, the stars sparkling in the distance the only witness. When he reached for her, Abby moved into his arms with no hesitation. Encircling his neck, she kissed him with abandon, letting her love consume them both.

Dev let go of the side to hold her and they sank beneath the water.

Laughing and splashing, they surfaced.

"That's one way to cool off," she said, grabbing for the side.

"Let's move to the shallow end," he said, kicking away and swimming to the other end of the pool on his back, his gaze never leaving hers.

Abby followed slowly. She was playing with wildfire, but she didn't care. This could be her last night in Texas. Why not spend it with the man she loved?

Dev was waiting when she swam to him, pulling her quickly into his arms to kiss her. His lips were cool, but quickly warmed. His tongue swept inside her mouth to tantalize and excite. Giving in to the ardor that arose, Abby traced the muscles in his shoulders, across his chest. Reveling in the sensations that filled her, she wished the moment could last a lifetime.

"I want you, Abby," Dev said, kissing a trail across her wet cheek. "Let's become lovers."

Her heart stopped, skipped a beat then raced.

Pulling back, she tried to see him, but he was silhouetted against the stars, she couldn't see into his eyes, judge his expression.

"Lovers?" she repeated, stunned.

"You're attracted to me, I'm attracted to you. There's something explosive between us, Abby. Let me come back to your apartment and make love to you."

For one glorious moment, Abby almost said yes. Dev wanted her. He wanted them to become lovers!

But reality crashed down. Dev had not mentioned *love*.

"You want to become lovers, does that mean fall in love, the whole bit?" she asked.

He shook his head, cradling her head in his palms. "I want you, Abby. More and more every time I see you. We're both single adults, unattached, uncommitted. Why not share this attraction? You can't deny you feel it, too."

"Attraction? Maybe what I feel is love," she said slowly, wishing she could see his expression, gauge how her words impacted him.

Dev's harsh laughter sounded loud in the quiet night. "Not you, too? I thought you were different. So now it's *love?*"

Abby disengaged herself from his hold and moved through the water to the steps. Climbing from the pool, she refused to give in to the incredible hurt his laughter and scornful words generated.

Picking up her towel, she wrapped it around sarong style and wrung the water from her hair. Amazed she was even functioning with the blossoming pain in her heart, she watched him warily as he followed her from the pool.

"So the answer is no?" Dev asked, keeping his distance.

"You know what, Dev? You're a very special person. And you deserve happiness. I hope you find it. But scoffing at the genuine feelings of others is not real conducive to that end. Is it so unbelievable that someone could fall in love with you? I think you are a wonderful man. I wish--"

She bit her lip and shook her head. "I wish things had been different, that's all. Good night."

Hurrying across the lawn, Abby felt numb. He wanted to

become lovers, but not be in love. How could she give herself to someone who refused to give a part of himself back?

Had she misjudged him? Was he not worthy of her love? Had she only loved an illusion?

She took a quick shower and climbed into bed. But it was almost morning before she fell asleep.

The next morning Abby finished breakfast before she saw Dev and Ruth walking toward the garage. A few minutes later they drove away. From the clothes they wore, and the time, she suspected they were going to church.

But not Sam.

This would be the perfect time to find Samuel Williams-- alone.

Without further thought, Abby headed down the stairs. Stopping in the shed to get some clippers, she cut an armful of flowers, keeping her eye on the time. She entered the house through the kitchen.

Thelma was absent. Mrs. Mitton sat reading the Sunday paper as she sipped from a cup of coffee.

"Good morning," she said, looking up at Abby and the flowers. "More flowers? I thought you filled every room."

"Just one more. Mrs. Williams said she liked filling the house with them." Hoping she looked more confident than she felt, she breezed through and into the main house. Pausing to listen carefully, she heard nothing. Taking a deep breath, she headed for the steps. She'd knock before entering the sitting room. And just maybe the connecting door would be open.

A noise from the office stopped her. Turning, she walked to the open door and peered inside.

An older man sat behind the desk, perusing some papers. He had a touch of silver at his temples and the weathered skin of someone who spent a lot of time out of doors. He looked a bit thin, but Abby attributed that to his recent illness. His clothes weren't that loose, attesting to the fact he was probably in good physical condition normally.

"Hello," she said, her heart in her throat.

He raised his head, hazel eyes looking quizzically at her. Abby tried to absorb every detail so she could tell Caroline and Michelle if he was the one.

"Hello, you must be Abby Brown, our new gardener. My wife said she met you yesterday. I'm Samuel Williams." He rose and smiled easily, holding out his hand.

Abby nodded, stepping inside and shaking his hand quickly.

"I thought you might like to have some flowers in here." She felt tongue-tied, shy, awkward. How did one go about asking a stranger if he were her father?

"That was thoughtful. I don't often have flowers in here."

Abby looked around. She had forgotten a vase.

"I'll be right back, I need a vase."

Fleeing to the kitchen, she tried to get control of her emotions. If the man was not her father, he'd think her a blithering idiot. And if he were, she wanted him to be interested enough to talk to her, not suspect she needed a keeper.

Taking a vase back into the office a few moments later, Abby set it on a bookcase and began to place flowers into it.

Sam had begun to read again. Should she talk? Or remain silent? She glanced at him, trying to see something that would tell her he was the one.

He looked up, leaned back in his chair.

"I understand you've been seeing Dev."

She blinked. That was the last thing she'd expected him to say.

"I'm not sure *seeing him* is the right phrase. We've spent a little time together. He was staying here, I have the garage apartment." She shrugged, not wanting to even think about Dev at this moment.

Samuel motioned Abby to sit down. She perched on the edge of one of the comfortable wing-back chairs near the window and watched him warily. Now what?

"Mrs. Mitton seems to feel differently. She spoke about it to Ruth."

"Oh." Abby looked at her hands trying to figure how to answer while wondering what exactly Mrs. Mitton had said.

"You're the first woman who's taken Dev's eye in a long time."

"Since Elizabeth, you mean?" she asked, looking at him.

"So he told you about Elizabeth?"

Abby nodded. "I think she really hit him hard."

"Nonsense, she was a blatant little gold digger looking for a free ride. He caught on to her before they tied the knot."

"Maybe not fast enough," she murmured, thinking of his

philosophy of marriage. A man who hadn't been burned badly would never consider he had to match bank accounts before he could trust his feelings.

"Have we met before?" Sam asked. He looked at her thoughtfully.

"I don't think so. I'm from New Orleans. Have you been there recently?"

He shook his head, still staring at her. "Not for many years. But there's something..."

"Have you lived in Texas your entire life?" she asked. She remembered what Dev had said, but would Sam tell her something different?

"Most of it. Came from Montana originally. Winters up there are too cold for me. I like the southern states."

"States? Have you lived in more than one?"

Was it her imagination, or had he grown more guarded? "A few. What brings you to Texas?"

You, Abby wanted to say, but her courage failed her. "Family."

She tried to find a resemblance between this man and her sisters or herself. Maybe the hair color was close to Caroline's. Maybe the jaw reminded her of Michelle's.

Or maybe she was just indulging in wishful thinking. She seemed to be doing it a lot lately.

"Here you are, Mr. Williams." Mrs. Mitton entered carrying a silver tray with coffee and sweet rolls. "Got to build back your strength and weight," she said, placing the tray on his desk.

"I can bring a cup for Abby if you like," she said, glancing at Abby.

"Do, we're chatting about things. I'm hoping she'll bring up my son soon," he said with a twinkle in his eye.

The housekeeper laughed. "You just wait until you see them together, then you'll know." She was still chuckling when she left the room.

"I don't need to stay," Abby said, jumping up. "I'll just finish the flowers and leave you to your coffee."

"Now don't run off. Ruth and Dev have gone to church and I'm alone in the house."

"Except for Mrs. Mitton and Thelma," Abby said, poking another stem into the vase.

"But I've known them for years. It's you I'm curious about. What have you and Dev been up to?"

"An afternoon at the beach and one party thrown by one of your vendors, hardly anything important."

"The Titan annual event? Isn't that interesting?"

She started to tell him interesting didn't describe things, that she had fallen in love with his stepson. But it was not his business. If Dev didn't believe her, why would anyone else?

Stuffing the last of the flowers into the vase, ignoring their ragged appearance, Abby gathered the cut ends and dumped them in the small trash can standing beside the desk.

Subtlety was obviously not her forte. She didn't know how to get the information she wanted without coming right out and asking.

"Did you ever live--"

Mrs. Mitton bustled in, carrying a cup of coffee. "I put cream in it like you drink it, Abby."

The phone rang.

Abby closed her mouth, reached for the cup and gave Mrs. Mitton a polite smile. "Thank you."

She tried to ignore Sam's side of the conversation as she sipped her coffee. When he hung up, she'd ask him if he had ever lived in Mississippi. If he said no, she'd let it go. Or would he say that anyway? Did he still believe there was a murder charge with his name on it? Wouldn't he have changed his name and tried to keep a low profile if that was the case? Yet if he knew the real murderer had been apprehended, why had he stayed away?

"That was my wife. She's joined friends for lunch. I'll need to tell Thelma," he said as he hung up the phone. "Unless you'd care to join us? Dev will be home in a few minutes. We eat at one."

"You'd ask the gardener to Sunday dinner?" she exclaimed before she could stop herself. Her grandmother never sat down a day in her life with the hired help. Even Rosalie, who'd worked for her for years.

"Not normally, but I think I'm inviting someone Dev's interested in."

I want you, Abby, Dev's words echoed in her mind. Was that interest?

"What do you say?" Sam asked.

"About what?" Dev stood in the doorway, his gaze fixed on Abby.

"Nothing." She jumped up and placed her cup and saucer on the edge of the desk, starting toward the door, anxious to escape. The last thing she planned to do was confront Sam in front of an audience. Throwing him a brief glance, she tried to smile. "Thanks anyway."

Dev didn't move. Abby couldn't get through the door with him blocking it.

"Excuse me."

"What are you doing here?" he asked suspiciously.

"I brought in some more flowers. Would you please move?"

He looked across the room at the vase with the haphazardly placed flowers. "Not as neat an arrangement as in the other rooms," he commented.

"So fix it yourself," she said, standing close enough to feel the heat of his body. "Would you move?" she said through her teeth.

The air almost shimmered between them. Abby longed to throw herself into his arms and have him hold her as if he'd never let her go. Did his stepfather suspect? How could anyone not pick up on the attraction they shared? It seemed to hum between them.

Dev had to pick up on it, too. He looked at her for a long moment, then stepped aside. When Abby hurried from the room, he kept pace with her, catching her arm near the bottom of the stairs and swinging her around to face him.

"I haven't changed my mind," he said, kissing her before she could say a word.

"Nor have I," she whispered when he raised his head. Involuntarily she brushed her fingertips against his lips and then turned to leave.

"Have dinner with me. We can talk," he said stiffly.

She glanced over her shoulder. He stood ramrod straight at the foot of the stairs, his expression schooled to reveal nothing.

I want you, Abby. He might as well have shouted it, she heard it echo so clearly in her mind.

"I think conversation would be futile."

"Have dinner with me," he practically ordered.

"And if I don't?"

A glimmer of amusement shone in his eyes. "I might have known it wouldn't be easy. Do you ever do anything the easy way?"

Warily she watched him. She was not answering that comment.

"I'll pick you up at seven," he said.

Without waiting for a response, he turned and went back to the den. A moment later she heard the murmur of the men's voices. Were they talking about her?

Abby followed Dev into the elevator of his apartment building shortly after seven that evening. The car whisked them quickly to the twentieth floor. The hall was spacious, quiet and empty. When he unlocked his door, he stood aside to allow her to enter.

Compared to her tiny apartment in Metairie, his place was palatial. The living room was comprised of a wall of windows giving a sweeping view of Houston and the tree covered landscape that extended as far as she could see. To the left she saw a small dining area and beyond that a kitchen.

"This is great," she said, examining everything, from the

landscapes pictures that adorned the walls, to the thick chocolate-brown carpeting underfoot. The sofa and chair were heavy Spanish style, solid and comfortable. The coffee table in front of the sofa showed signs of wear.

A large-screen television sat in the corner, beside a stereo setup that looked complicated. Business journals, newspapers were evident.

Abby turned around and smiled at him, hoping he couldn't tell how nervous she felt. "This looks like you. Solid and strong."

"That makes me sound like a plow horse."

"Would you rather be thought dashing and reckless?"

"Dashing's not bad. And I definitely feel reckless tonight, don't you?"

"A bit." Flustered by the look in his eye, she glanced toward the kitchen. "I smell something wonderful. What's for dinner?"

"Shish kebab, wild rice and a salad. Chocolate mousse for dessert."

She looked at him, her eyes widening. "Wow, I didn't know you could cook. That sounds terrific!"

He inclined his head once.

Something about it clued her in.

"Did you cook it?" she asked suspiciously.

"It's in my kitchen, why wouldn't I cook it?"

"You didn't prepare it, did you?" she guessed.

"Doesn't warming it up count as cooking?"

Abby laughed. "Thelma?"

"Trust me, Abby, you wouldn't want to try my cooking.

I'm pretty good at boiling water, but somehow miss the nuances of cooking more than one thing and having everything ready at the same time."

Her smile faded and she studied him. "I do trust you, Dev. The thing is I think you need to trust yourself."

He walked into the kitchen. Abby followed, standing against the island counter watching as he checked the oven.

"You said we'd talk," she reminded him.

"We will, but let's eat first."

Like the lull before the storm, Abby thought.

"Okay. What can I do to help?"

For the next few minutes they worked together companionably in the small kitchen. If he brushed against her more frequently than was strictly necessary, she didn't mind. Each touch brought a new shiver of awareness and growing anticipation.

If she bumped into him a couple of times, it was accidental, despite how much she liked his hands coming up to steady her. For a little while she let herself imagine them preparing dinner together every night. They wouldn't have to rely on Thelma's cooking, Abby could cook.

They'd eat, talk over their day, then retire to the bedroom and close the world behind them.

It was a lovely daydream, she thought as he seated her at the table. Candles had been lit, the places set beside each other. When he dimmed the overhead light, Abby realized how romantic the man could be. Did he have a clue? It was delightful for a woman to feel so cherished.

Yet always in the back of her mind was the looming talk. Would they clear the air or only confuse things even more?

Chapter Nine

Dev ate slowly, watching Abby. She seemed on edge, but he couldn't fault that. He'd caused it with his blatant invitation last night. Even now, he wasn't certain why she'd refused. She was attracted to him. He knew that from her flirtatious looks, the touches in the kitchen, the way she blushed sometimes when he looked at her.

And all of it made him want her even more.

But he wasn't falling for the love fallacy. Why did women want to hear some undying commitment before giving in to their own needs? He wanted her, she wanted him, it was simple. Neither had anyone it'd hurt.

Unless she was holding out for something more. She wouldn't be the first woman to withhold sex to get her way.

"This is delicious," Abby said.

"I'll let Thelma know you like it." He smiled.

She'd seen right through his deception. Not that he truly wanted her to believe he could cook. Honesty was important in any relationship.

Blast it, there was that word again.

"Why the frown?" she asked. "Don't you like it?"

"Just a disquieting thought."

When she resumed eating he watched her. It felt right to be eating with her. To work in the kitchen together.

But feeling right tonight and a long-term commitment were two vastly different things.

As far as he knew, she didn't have any money. Was she hoping to change that by luring him into some kind of relationship? Were all women like Elizabeth?

Or was Abby different?

Dev suggested they take their coffee and brandy into the living room after stacking the dishes in the sink when they'd finished eating. Sinking down on the comfortable sofa, Abby half turned toward him, tucking her feet up on the cushions.

"So let's have it," she said. "We've eaten and if I have to end up walking home, I don't want it to be too late."

He sat beside her, close enough to touch her knees, her breasts almost brushing against his arm. She wanted to talk and he wanted to kiss her, hold her, make love to her. Be surrounded by Abby until he forgot the rest of the world and could only see her.

"You're not going to be walking home. I'll take you. The question is when."

"When?"

"Tonight--or tomorrow morning?"

He watched the color rise in her cheeks. Touching her cheek lightly with his fingertips, he expected to be scorched, but she was only warm.

She held his gaze. Dev knew enough about poker to know when to hold. He'd made his interest clear. The next move was up to her. Though if he didn't know better, he'd almost suspect she was shy. But no woman reached her age without having some involvement with men. No doubt this contrary woman would surprise him with her response.

"Tonight, then," she said almost sadly.

Dev sighed and leaned his head back against the cushions, closing his eyes. "Damn," he said softly.

She giggled.

Opening his eyes, he rolled his head to the right to glare at her. "It's not funny."

"I'm nervous. I've never had someone want me so much."

"What do you mean never? Are the men in New York blind?"

She smiled broadly, catching her lower lip between her teeth. That almost sent Dev through the roof. He'd like to tug gently on that full lower lip with his own teeth, cover her mouth with his and taste the sweet delight he'd found before.

"You're terrific for a woman's ego," she said, lightly tracing a pattern on his cheek with a fingertip.

Dev reached up and clasped her hand, bringing it down and lacing his fingers through hers. Her palm was warm, her hand small in his, yet capable. She was nothing like Elizabeth. Dare he risk more than a casual involvement?

"But I can't," she said, her eyes gravely serious. "We both have things in the way--you with your hang-up about people liking you only because of the money. And me--well, I have something to tell you, but you're going to be furious. Will this attraction we feel be strong enough to last?"

Dev's heart sank. She was married.

"Tell me, and see."

"Not tonight. This is just for us. We can spend a few hours together, then you can take me home and come back here in plenty of time to get a good night's sleep for work tomorrow."

He shook his head. "I don't need a lot of sleep. Stay."

He could see the hesitation, almost feel the warring factions within her. Part of her wanted to, he was sure of that. Maybe she was playing hard to get.

She tugged her hand, but he refused to release her. He wanted the close contact, wanted to know how she felt as her expression changed. Wanted to make her desire him as much as he desired her.

"If you're married, just go ahead and say it!" he ordered.

"Married? Me? No, I'm not married. I just finished my training. I sure didn't have time to get married."

"Training? To be a gardener?"

He didn't examine the sense of relief her words brought. She was single, just as he was.

Pulling gently, he tumbled her off balance and against his chest. His arms pulled her close and his mouth found hers with unerring instinct. Despite her reluctance to become involved, her kiss was hot and exciting. She held nothing back and he threaded his fingers through her hair, holding her while he traced her lips then slipped between them with his tongue. She was sweet as natural honey, warm as the Texas sun.

And his.

He just had to convince her of that fact.

Slowly Abby shook her head and pulled back.

"Dev, we'd better stop. I'm trying to do what I think's right, but you don't make it easy for me to even remember my own name."

She pushed away and stood up, trying to straighten her dress, avoiding his gaze.

He debated arguing with her. But tonight wasn't the only night they'd have together. Her kiss had been as passionate as anything he'd ever experienced. Maybe he could play her waiting game.

But not patiently.

Rising, he towered over her, frustration filling him.

"How long will this go on?"

"What?" she asked, stepping back, bumping the coffee table. Her purse fell on the far side, its contents spilling across the rug.

"Playing hot and cold. You're not indifferent. You may say one thing, but your lips don't lie when we kiss. You want me, too."

"Yes, you're right. But for different reasons."

Her words from the night before echoed in his mind. *Maybe what I feel is love.*

"I don't love you. I've never pretended that I do," Dev said.

"I know. I never asked you to say it."

"But you want me to," he pushed, his frustration growing.

She shrugged, trying to act indifferent, but he could see

the hurt in her eyes. "You've done nothing to lead me on. Good heavens, you practically wear a sign saying you distrust all women. If I fell in love, that's my business. But I do have to protect myself any way I can, and making love with you would make it twice as hard to walk away afterward."

The thought of her walking away almost forced a denial from him. He didn't want her leaving. He wanted to be able to see her every day, watch her eyes light up when he entered a room, track the color as it flushed her cheeks when he teased her. Wanted to share her passion in the night, and her sunny disposition each morning.

Was he falling in love with Abby Brown despite all his efforts to the contrary?

"I'd better go," she said. Looking around, she spotted her purse and contents.

Dev rounded the table and began to gather things up and hand them to her. Abby stuffed them into her purse.

When he picked up her wallet, she reached out to snatch it from his hand. It fell open--her Louisiana driver's license clearly displayed.

"Give me that," she said, reaching for it again.

Dev swung around, moving it out of her reach as he captured her hand in his. He read the license again.

Talmadge? Where had he heard that name before?

Swinging back he stared at her.

"Who are you?" he asked.

Abby cleared her throat, her expression similar to a deer caught in headlights, terrified, yet mesmerized, unable to move.

His eyes fixed on hers, he saw her take a deep breath, slowly exhale.

"I'm Abby Talmadge. My sisters and I think Sam Williams may be our father."

"Well, he isn't. What scam are you trying to run?"

"Let me explain, Dev," she said in her normal Southern drawl. There was no use for pretense any longer. She watched his eyes widen in disbelief. "Just listen for a minute! I told you I have two sisters, older sisters. Our mother died shortly after I was born. I've seen pictures of her, but don't remember a thing about her. And there were no pictures of our father. Grandmother destroyed all of them."

"You were an orphan and your grandmother raised all three girls, I remember. But what does that have to do with your being here and claiming my father is yours?"

"Actually, that's only part right. I'm not an orphan. I think I have a father living. My brother-in-law Josh is a private investigator and he narrowed down the list to three men. The one in New Jersey isn't the right man. Now it's down to two. Your step-father might be the one."

"I thought you said your father had died."

"I said, he'd gone before my mother. I let you think I meant he died, but what I meant was literally that--he'd gone before my mother died. Gone, left, disappeared. All my life I thought he'd abandoned us before I was even born. But we found out last spring that he hadn't left of his own volition. He'd been forced to leave or face a murder charge."

"Your father committed a *murder*?"

She shook her head. "Of course not. I should have said

face a *bogus* murder charge. It's long and involved and complicated and I don't want to go into it all right now. But the fact is he was forced to leave because of my grandmother's interference. She wanted her only daughter to marry into an old Louisiana family with a lengthy heritage and lots of money."

"Louisiana?"

"Caroline found out most of the story when she and Brandon cleared up our grandmother's estate. Michelle married Josh so he'd help us locate our father. And I'm here because we think we have."

Dev glared at her. His grip tightened convulsively on her hand.

"Suddenly it all makes sense. The endless questions. The fascination with my upbringing. You're that woman who phoned me at the office and tried to convince me you're my stepfather's daughter."

He wanted to throw something. Howl at the moon! Blast everything! He'd begun to care for Abby Brown.

"Your name isn't Abby Brown. So let me guess, you're not a gardener either."

She shook her head. "A nurse."

"How dare you try to worm your way into our home, our lives, to set yourself up as a long-lost daughter! What happened? Did you see that as a long shot once you heard he was doing better? Decide getting involved with me offered a better chance? Easier to have me make a play for you than convince my father he has a daughter?"

"Actually, three daughters," Abby said, trying to pry his hand from hers. "Let me go, Dev."

"Get your purse, we're leaving. You can pack your bags tonight and hit the road. The deception didn't work. You're lucky I don't call the police. I may yet."

She finally pulled her hand free.

"I didn't expect to fall in love with you. Please listen to me."

He shook his head. "The time for talking is over. We'll take a full inventory of everything in the house. If anything is missing you'll be our first suspect."

Abby stood, her chin raised, her eyes glaring right back at him. "Nothing's missing, and I'm not leaving until I find out for sure if this Samuel Williams is my father."

"*This* Samuel Williams? How many are there?"

"If you'd been listening you would have heard me a minute ago. Josh narrowed the list to three. We didn't have a lot to go on. Apparently Sam Williams worked for Sinjin Oil out of New Orleans at one time. The company records were burned, but Josh thought one of the three men was the right one. He checked out the one in New Jersey, Brandon is checking on the one in California, I drew Texas."

"Nice try, lady, but I've already answered your questions. My dad is not the man you're looking for. Try your scam somewhere else."

"Ask him," she said. "Just ask him. Or let me."

"No way, get your things, we're leaving." He handed her the wallet.

"Dev, this doesn't finish it. One way or another, sooner or later, Josh or Brandon or I will speak with your father. You can be present, or not, your choice. But I deserve to know for sure. My sisters deserve to know. And maybe even our father would believe he deserves to know. We don't understand why he stayed away, but whatever the reason, we *deserve* to know."

"I'll call your bluff," Dev said, reaching out to pick up a phone. He quickly dialed.

"Hi, Mom, is Dad around? No, just wanted to check something with him." He held Abby's gaze, covering the mouthpiece while he waited. "What was your mother's name?"

"Ask him if he knew Amanda Talmadge from Baton Rouge."

"Hi, Dad. I've got a woman here who claims to be your long-lost daughter. She says to ask you if you ever knew an Amanda Talmadge from Baton Rouge."

Dev felt his world tilt when his father replied.

"She was my first wife. We had two daughters. I haven't seen them in more than twenty years. Which one is looking for me? Bring her by the house, son."

"We'll be right there," Dev said slowly. He hung up, his eyes still locked with Abby's.

Her gaze became compassionate. She reached out as if to touch him, then dropped her hand. Tears began to fill her eyes.

"He's my father, isn't he?" she asked, biting her lower lip when it began to tremble. "My whole life I've missed having a daddy. Now I've found him, haven't I?"

"So it appears."

He'd been wrong, she *was* exactly like Elizabeth. Once

again, he hadn't been what a woman had wanted--only the means to an end.

When Dev pulled into the driveway, he drove straight to the front door, not stopping by the garage. Every light on the ground floor seemed to be on. The outside lights as well. He stopped the car at the foot of the steps.

"So the prodigal returns," he said scathingly.

Abby looked at him. "Not exactly. But I do want to talk to him. I'm not taking away your father. I'm only claiming mine."

"We'll see exactly what you're after, won't we?"

He opened his door and headed for the house. Abby watched him pass the front of the car and recognized his deliberate lack of manners as the slap he no doubt intended.

Had she gained a father and lost a love?

No, she thought pragmatically as she opened her door and stepped out, she'd never had the love.

Before Dev could open the front door it swung wide, Ruth and Samuel stood in the light.

Abby stopped dead, scared. She wished her sisters were with her.

"Dad, Mom, meet Abby Talmadge. Apparently a long-lost daughter."

Samuel glanced at Dev, hearing the bitterness in his tone. Then he looked at Abby.

"I don't have a daughter named Abby."

"Actually, you do," she said, climbing the shallow steps. "I was born seven months after you were driven away by Eugenia Talmadge. Caroline and Michelle are my older sisters. Amanda Talmadge was my mother. How do you do?" She held out her hand, hoping no one noticed how it shook.

Samuel hesitated only a second before enfolding her into his arms.

She felt Ruth hug them both.

"Oh, Samuel, one of your daughters! I'm so happy for you, my love," she said softly.

Samuel eased Abby back until he held her shoulders. Gazing into her eyes, he nodded. "I should have known instantly when we talked earlier. You have a look of your mother."

"That's why I seemed familiar?"

"Your eyes are just like Amanda's."

"As are Caroline's and Michelle's. We don't look alike except for the Talmadge eyes."

"I can't believe I never heard of you. Amanda should have told me she was pregnant. She owed me that much at least."

"Maybe we should go sit down, darling. I'm sure we all want to hear everything. And Abby probably has questions as well," Ruth said, closing the door, glancing at her son.

"I have plenty of questions myself," Dev said, his arms folded, his expression once again impassive. "And not just for Abby."

He was blazing angry, she knew. But she had more than she could deal with at the moment with her own emotions.

Her *father* had his arm around her shoulders. Her *father* was walking with her into his living room.

166 | BARBARA MCMAHON

Samuel and Ruth exchanged a look. "I'm sure you do, son. It could be a long evening. Ask Thelma to fix us a pot of coffee and bring something to eat," Samuel said as he passed with Abby in the circle of his arm.

Ten minutes later they were settled in the living room. Sam sat on the sofa beside Abby, Ruth in a chair flanking the sofa. Dev remained standing near one of the windows--apart, as if distancing himself from the rest of them.

Abby looked at him. She didn't want to change things with his family. But she knew he'd see her as a threat to the stability he and his parents had enjoyed since Samuel married Ruth all those years ago.

"I wasn't sure you'd want to acknowledge me," Abby said, looking at her father. She wanted to ask him why he'd had no contact with his daughters, but didn't want to aggravate the tenuous situation.

"Honey, I didn't even know about you. I could kill your mother. She should have told me."

Abby looked at him oddly. "My mother has been dead for twenty-two years. I was six weeks old when she died."

"What?" Samuel exclaimed.

"You're only twenty-two?" Dev said.

"We didn't know she'd died," Ruth said with a quelling glance at her son. "Maybe you should explain things to her, Samuel, let her know what happened. I'm sure Abby has a million questions. We can ask her ours when we've answered hers."

"We know some of what happened," Abby said. "My grandmother died earlier this year--in February. She was ill for several weeks before her death and Caroline cared for her. Something she said made Caroline suspicious. She and Brandon found out you'd been falsely accused of a crime and threatened with prison. That's why you left, right?"

"A murder charge. Thanks to Eugenia. Amanda and I had been having trouble in our marriage--ever since we settled at Talmadge Hall. The threat of a trial and prison was more than she could take. I couldn't convince her the charges were false. We had a fight and I left."

He shook his head. "I always thought it'd be temporary. Tempers were high. And your grandmother was a fearful opponent. I didn't know how to fight her. She had money, a name, influential friends. And her daughter's love."

Samuel looked at Ruth. She smiled encouragingly.

"I received a letter from Amanda saying she wanted a divorce and planned to ask for full custody of our daughters. I only knew about Caroline and Michelle."

"So she knew where to find you?" Abby asked.

"She knew. She wrote several times. The last letter told me she was marrying somebody there in Baton Rouge once our divorce was final. She asked me to never contact her again."

"Not even to see your daughters?"

"I've thought a lot over the years that I should have fought harder. But at the time I was out of work, had no money, no way to fight your grandmother. She had threatened to provide proof that I had killed a man. I wouldn't have had a chance in Baton Rouge against her. When I got Amanda's last letter, I gave up. I'd gone back to working the rigs in the Gulf. The pay was great, but there was no way I could do that and have two little girls stay with me--even occasionally. Besides, I know what it's like to be dragged back and forth between warring parents. I didn't want that for my daughters. Amanda assured me the girls would be better off having one father figure, the man she was marrying."

"She never married anyone else. Never, as far as we can ascertain, even looked at another man. And she died so soon after I was born, she didn't have a chance to do much of anything," Abby said slowly.

"I didn't even know she was dead," he said. "All these years..."

"Someone must have told you. Why would you have married Ruth?"

"I got a letter a year after I left from Judge Hargraves. He said I was free to marry again, then proceeded to warn me to stay away from Baton Rouge if I knew what was good for me. I always figured it was a guilty conscience on his part. He'd backed Eugenia Talmadge when she threatened my arrest."

Abby felt overwhelmed. Her grandmother was responsible for much more than just separating her daughter from her husband.

"But Caroline and Michelle must have known I cared. I sent cards every year at Christmas and their birthdays. I had to send them to Talmadge Hall since I didn't have Amanda's new address. To this day I've never set foot in Louisiana. But I invited both Caroline and then Michelle to visit me when they each turned eighteen. When they didn't respond, I thought Amanda had been correct, they were better without me in their life."

"They never got any cards," Abby said slowly. That she knew for a fact. "Eugenia must have intercepted them."

"All these years, lost," Samuel murmured. "Because of pride."

"Pride?"

"I wanted Amanda to come to me on my terms. I wanted her to prove to me that our love was stronger than the ties to her mother. She had to know I'd never murder anyone. I stayed away when I should have confronted them all."

"My sisters and I have speculated that she'd have left her mother and gone after you, but that last pregnancy was hard and then she died so soon afterward," Abby said gently.

"Amanda's letters?" Ruth asked.

Abby shook her head. "I can only guess they came from Eugenia. What's a forged letter or two after everything else she'd done. And that definitely is an example of pride. She wanted a prestigious alliance for Amanda, and refused to let anything stand in her way. Except my mother's death. If it makes you feel any better, she tried the same thing with Caroline and her marriage."

"Tell me all about Caroline and Michelle and you. We have a lifetime to catch up on," Samuel said eagerly, reaching out to clasp her hand in both of his.

"If you will excuse me, I'll head for home. I don't need to hear any more. I have work to do and a full day at the office tomorrow," Dev said, pushing away.

Samuel looked up. "Stay a while longer, son. I need to explain to you why your mother and I never mentioned my first marriage. We--"

"I don't need an explanation. It's obviously something you didn't want to talk about." He headed for the door.

"Dev, wait!" Samuel rose and followed his son into the foyer. With a hasty word to Ruth, Abby followed right behind them.

"This changes nothing between us, Dev. You're still my son," Samuel was saying when she reached the foyer.

For a long moment Dev held his gaze, then nodded once, briefly.

"If you say so."

"You're my son in every way that counts, the only child I helped to raise. I've always been proud of you. I'll always love you. This doesn't affect our relationship."

"Thanks, Dad."

"Dev, wait," Abby said.

"We have nothing to talk about," he said. With a quick expressionless glance at her, he was gone.

"Dev!"

Chapter Ten

Abby stared at the closed door in disbelief for a long moment before meeting the sympathetic gaze in her father's eyes.

"Let him go, honey. He'll be back. This has been as big a shock to him as it is to me. Give him some time to get used to things. Come and tell me all about you and your sisters."

Abby longed to run after Dev. They'd resolved nothing. She knew he was angry. Would he even listen to her? Would it be better to talk to him later, when he'd had time to cool down, or now, before he could build barriers and find a reason to avoid ever seeing her again?

This should be one of the happiest days of her life. She'd found her father!

But somehow the excitement she'd anticipated had dimmed. She longed for Dev. She wanted to explain, make sure he understood.

Make sure he could forgive her deception.

Would he ever kiss her again? Repeat his request to become lovers?

"Dev will come around," Samuel said as they went back into the living room. "Now, tell me everything, leave nothing out! Ruth, do you want to stay up with us?"

"I wouldn't miss this for the world!" she said, her smile warm and full of love.

Hoping Sam knew his stepson well, that Dev *would* come around, Abby sat back down and began to tell her father about growing up in Baton Rouge, the fun she and Caroline and Michelle shared, the disappointments. But she kept back the emotions that resulted from never knowing their father. Tonight should be happy, not a time for recriminations and regrets.

She could hardly wait to learn more about what Samuel had done over the years. And then call her sisters.

They talked until well after midnight. Abby knew she should let Caroline and Michelle know she'd found their father, but it was too late by the time she reached her garage apartment. She could hardly wait until tomorrow.

Early the next morning, Abby called Michelle.

"It's him," she said simply.

"What--your Sam Williams is our father?" Michelle exclaimed. "How did you find out? Does he know who you are? Did he ask after me and Caroline? How is he? What does he look like? Do you like him? Does he want to see us? I can't believe you found him! It's actually him? How did you do it?"

"Yes, it's him. And I didn't precisely do it. Dev forced the issue."

For a moment the pain of his rejection rose and threatened her newfound happiness. She still had to speak with him, clear the air. See where she stood--if anywhere.

But first she needed to take care of family business.

"Dev? How did that happen?"

"He saw my name on my driver's license and threatened to call the police. He thought I was trying some scam to get money out of the family. But I insisted he ask his father if he had ever known Amanda Talmadge. I think Dev was more surprised than I was when Samuel said our mother had been his first wife."

Abby paused a moment, trying to catch her breath. It still seemed surreal.

"He was glad to see me, Michelle. Samuel. That's what they call him now, not Sam. And he wrote to you and Caroline for years. He even invited you both to visit when you each turned eighteen. The worst was he didn't know our mother had died."

Michelle demanded details and Abby spent over an hour recounting everything she could remember from the previous evening.

Except for Dev's reaction. His leaving without a word. That still hurt, and was too personal to share even with her sister.

When she wound down, Michelle said, "You haven't said anything about his stepson. How's he taking it? Is he bent out of shape to find he's not an only child anymore?"

Trust Michelle to pick up on that omission.

Abby swallowed, blinking against the threat of tears. "He was mad. At me. And at his parents. They'd never told him about us. I suspect he's also hurt. Samuel trusts him enough to leave his company in his hands, raised him as a father, but never told him about his first wife and family."

"Why not?"

"I asked him that. He said Dev was too young at the time he married Ruth. And when Caroline and you didn't take him up on his invitation to visit, he thought it best to just let the past rest. My turning up was quite a shock. A happy one, he keeps telling me."

"What's he like?"

"You'll see for yourself soon. I'm returning home in a couple of days. Samuel and Ruth are planning to come to New Orleans next week. We figured I could go with you to break the news to Caroline and then she'll be prepared when she meets them."

"Wow, I'm still in shock," Michelle said.

"Yeah, me too. Go tell Josh and then Brandon. But don't any of you dare tell Caroline until I get there!"

Abby hung up and glanced around. Another day or two to visit, to try to bridge twenty-two years apart, then she'd truly have to return home. She had a job to get back to. And nothing was holding her in Houston.

Samuel and Ruth had urged her to move into a guest room, but she'd asked to remain in the apartment over the garage. If Dev came looking for her, she wanted him to know where she was. And it would just be for another couple of days.

She couldn't wait to see Caroline's face when she told her. What an amazing journey, from discovering he hadn't abandoned them to actually finding him and learning he'd thought Amanda had rejected him.

By Thursday morning, Abby knew Dev wasn't coming.

She'd waited each day, hoping he'd call or stop by. She delayed her return home twice.

Samuel went into the office for a few hours every morning. He'd mention Dev at dinner each evening, reassuring Ruth that Dev would come around soon. And then he'd turn and question Abby. He was still catching up on every aspect of her life.

Nothing was ever said about the strained relations between Abby and Dev.

But then neither Samuel nor Ruth had known the extent of their interaction.

Both Samuel and Ruth urged her to consider staying with them indefinitely. She could obtain a job as a nurse at one of the local hospitals and live with them. "Give me a chance to get to know my youngest daughter," Samuel said.

She was happy to share her past and learn more about her father. But moving to Houston was more than she cared to consider at this time. Her family and her friends were in New Orleans. Everyone who meant anything to her.

Except for Dev.

Each day stretched out endlessly without a word from him. How awkward things would be if she truly considered accepting her father's invitation.

It was better to return home. The sooner she resumed her normal routine, the sooner she'd get over Dev.

She shivered. That made the future seem awfully bleak.

"We'll see about that!" she said, jumping to her feet. It'd been four days. She was leaving tomorrow. She had her plane tickets and her bags packed.

But Abby wasn't going home without seeing Dev first. He'd listen to what she had to say if she had to hog tie him to do so. And if she meant anything to him, he'd have to understand.

She dressed with care, donning the suit she'd worn when she first arrived in Houston, when she thought things would be so easy--walk into the office, ask to see Sam Williams and figure out if he was her father or not.

It felt like a lifetime ago.

As she backed her rental car from the driveway, she let her gaze wander over the yard. She hadn't killed anything except the plants she ran over with the mower. At least that was a plus. She knew with proper care, the yard would be a show-place.

When she reached the tower that housed the company's offices, she took the elevator to the top floor. Before she spoke to Dev, she wanted to see her father's office. He wasn't expecting her, but seemed delighted when his secretary ushered her in.

"Come to see where your dad works?" he asked, proudly introducing her to his secretary.

She nodded, smiling brightly. "I didn't get any trips here as a youngster. Don't kids usually visit where their parents work? Wow, this is great." The office was spacious, with windows on two walls.

"I'd probably never get anything done with a view like this," she said walking over to one of the windows. She felt shaky inside. Was she really interested in seeing this office or was it a stalling technique to put off her visit to Dev's?

"Want me to show you around?" Samuel asked, coming to stand beside her.

"No, thanks. I just wanted to see where you work. I'm on my way to talk to Dev before I head for home."

Samuel rubbed his chin, shook his head. "The boy's riding a grudge, honey. He's as mad at us as he is at you. Ruth and I did what we thought best under the circumstances. You'd think he could see that."

Abby smiled sadly at her father's soft Texas drawl and choice of words. "He's hardly a boy."

Samuel nodded. "I know. But I often think back to when Dev was a tough defensive teenager longing for happiness and so afraid to trust anyone."

"And Elizabeth did nothing to strengthen his concept of trust. Or me. But I still want to tell him goodbye."

"Don't go, honey. You know Ruth and I'd love to have you stay with us."

"I know," Abby said smiling warmly at her father. "And I appreciate the offer. But my home's in New Orleans. My new job's there. Besides, I can't wait to tell Caroline. She remembers you, you know. She'll be so thrilled."

"You'll have to come visit often. You and your sisters. And I'll have to meet their husbands, see that cute Penny you're always talking about."

She nodded. They'd discussed this a million times since Sunday night. But she thought it gave her father pleasure to speak of his daughters, to imagine becoming a part of their lives after all the years apart.

"I might just visit every couple of months."

Wouldn't Dev love that!

Two minutes later she opened the door to Dev's office. Samuel had overridden his secretary's objections to Abby's slipping in unannounced.

He sat at his computer screen, staring at a spreadsheet of numbers. Abby's heart caught. He looked tired. Had he been having trouble sleeping at night?

She sure had.

"Hi, Dev," she said softly.

He spun around. For a moment she thought he'd stand, but he relaxed and leaned back in his chair, watching her warily.

"What are you doing here?"

"I came to see you."

"Why? I think we said all we had to say a few nights ago."

She leaned against the door. His office wasn't as large as his father's, but he still seemed a million miles away.

"I'm sorry for the deception. At first I didn't think it'd matter. I was harming no one and really wanted to find out if Samuel was my father. But as we became friends--"

"Friends? Is that what you call it?" he interrupted.

"I thought we were friends. Or becoming friends."

If she had said yes, they could have become lovers.

"I don't need your type of friendship. You got what you want, why bother me anymore?"

"I don't mean to bother you, I just came to say goodbye."

He went still. "Goodbye?"

"I'm leaving. Since you seem to be avoiding your parents while I'm there, I didn't think you'd be dropping by their home any time soon. So I came here to say goodbye."

Slowly he stood, still watching her closely.

"And where are you going? Home to pack up?"

She shook her head. Pushing away from the door, she walked to the window. He shared some of his father's view. Hoping she looked casual and at ease, she glanced at him over her shoulder.

"I'm returning to New Orleans. I have a new job starting soon. And I want to be the one to tell my sister Caroline about our father."

He stepped around the desk, almost crowding her when he stopped. "What game are you playing now? I know Dad asked you to move in with him and Mom."

"And do you begrudge me a chance to get to know my father? It wasn't my fault or his that we don't know one another. You've had him for a long time. A few days isn't too much to ask, is it?"

"Not if it gets you all you want."

She smiled and nodded, swallowing hard against the tears that threatened.

"It did. I have a father who didn't voluntarily abandon me. Who even seems to like me. And your mother is a darling woman. She's so delighted in his happiness. I can't wait for them to meet Michelle and Caroline. I'm just sorry you and I have to part this way. I never meant to hurt you."

"A man has to care before he can be hurt."

She nodded again, staring out the window, hoping to hold off the tears.

He hadn't cared, he'd made that plain.

"Anyway, I'm sorry for the deception. But, I'd do it again, to find my father."

"The end justifies the means, no matter what? So you use me to get your own way, then say sorry and move on?"

"I didn't expect to fall in love!" she said, almost shouting as she turned to face him. "Which was dumb on my part, right? You told me from the very first you were not interested. This time tomorrow, I'll be gone and your life will resume its normal course. You can see your folks and do whatever you want. I won't *bother* you again. It won't be too hard to come up with reasons to stay away from Houston. And Samuel can see all three of his daughters by coming to New Orleans."

"If you play your cards right, I'm sure Samuel would keep open his offer to let you stay at the house. Wouldn't you like a bit of the glamour of being Samuel Williams' daughter? You could go to parties like the Titans put on, buy designer clothes, take exotic vacations. Money's no object."

Incensed, Abby clenched her hands into fists.

"You don't get it, do you? It was never about the *money*. It was about *family*. But if you can't see that, if you can't trust your father and mother and even yourself, then there's no explaining things to you. You know what? You remind me of my grandmother. She only saw things as they related to money, old family names, and prestige. Nothing else mattered. I'd be careful of that kind of thinking, if I were you. It can leave you alone and bitter in your old age."

Abby turned and headed for the door. This meeting had been a mistake. There was nothing left for them to say.

Dev beat her to the door, and held it closed with one hand. Looming over her, he looked down into her blue eyes.

"What can you do to prove me wrong?"

She studied him. Why was he asking? What *could* she do to prove him wrong?

Slowly she released her grip on the doorknob.

"Only time will prove that, Dev. I can promise I'll never tell another lie. But you'd have to know me for a lifetime to see if I keep that promise. I can tell you I love you and would never do anything to hurt you, but again, it would take a lifetime to prove it. You want everything wrapped up in guarantees from the get-go. Life isn't that way. Sometimes you just make a blind leap of faith, hold on and trust that everything will turn out the way you want."

"Are you suggesting *I* should make a blind leap of faith and trust *you* for a lifetime?"

She nodded. "I'd trust you with everything I have. You can trust me, too."

"I want to let you walk out of this office. I want to show you that you can't waltz into a man's life and turn it upside down and get away with it. I want to be strong enough to stand up to your leaving. And be able to tell myself years down the road that my life was better because of it."

He brushed her cheek with the back of his fingers.

"But I can't. These last few days have been hell. One minute I'm so angry with you I can hardly stand it. Then I remember your wide-eyed innocent look, how you delight in listening to my childhood memories, how you can make me forget the rest of the world with just a brush of your hand, or a sudden smile--and I think only of you. Of the laughter that lurks in your eyes, the soft feel of your skin, the sensations of coming home that I get whenever I'm with you."

"Oh, Dev," Abby whispered, almost afraid to breathe.

"The thought of you flying back to New Orleans and my not seeing you again is more than I wish to live with. So maybe I'll have to take you up on that lifetime of observations. I'll just make sure not to give you cause to lie and see if I can trust you as much as you trust me."

"I'll sign a prenuptial agreement and everything," she said quickly. "I don't want any of your money. I make enough as a nurse to support myself and will pay my share of the household."

Dev laughed, picked her up and spun her around and around.

"Maybe you make enough now, but when the babies come? Don't you want to stay home and watch them grow? Then where would you get money? I think maybe part of my trust has to start with commitment without a prenup. I love you, Abby Brown Talmadge. I want you to marry me and have my babies. Just think, we'll be one couple who never has in-law problems! Want to give it a try? Want to let me verify that you'll never lie that you'll always love me? Because I know I love you and always will."

"Yes, please," she said as he slowly lowered her to the floor and drew her into his arms.

His kiss was pure bliss. Abby had come home, too.

November

"Don't get tangled in the veil," Michelle warned Penny.

"I'm not, I want to see Auntie Abby all around," Penny said carefully watching where she put her feet. She beamed up at Abby.

"You looks pretty, Auntie Abby," she said.

"You do look lovely," Caroline said, sitting on one of the chairs.

Abby inclined her head regally. "Thank you," she said, gazing into the full-length mirror while Michelle straightened her veil. She smiled dreamily.

"Hasn't this been a wonderful year? Three brides in a row. I can't believe it."

Penny went to lean against Caroline and patted her rounded stomach. "My mommy's gonna have a baby, too, like you, Auntie Caroline. Then I'll have a sister or brother to play with."

"What?" Abby spun around.

Caroline sat up and stared at Michelle, her smile wide and delighted.

"Oh, Penny, sweetie, that was supposed to be a secret," Michelle said, laughing. She looked at Abby apologetically. "I didn't want to take anything away from your big day. We were going to tell you after the honeymoon."

184 | Barbara McMahon

"Oh, Michelle, how wonderful!" She hugged her sister. "That takes nothing away, for heaven's sakes, it adds to my happiness. Wow, I'm going to be an aunt three times over! Wouldn't you know it, just when I'm moving away, too."

"Congratulations, Michelle. I'm so happy for you. And Abby, Houston isn't that far," Caroline said, struggling to get up from the chair.

"Are you sure you're all right?" Abby asked when Caroline joined her sisters. The three looked at each other in the mirror. Abby had insisted on a traditional wedding, with formal gowns, attendants and a church ceremony. She only planned to marry once and wanted it to be a never-forgotten event. Thankfully the old church in Baton Rouge they'd attended as children helped to arrange everything. It was amazing what could be accomplished in 90 days.

"I'm fine. In a minute Dad will knock and it'll be time for us to go," Caroline said, massaging her lower back.

"Dad," Abby said with a smile. "That's another miracle of the year. I'll be forever sorry he wasn't around while we were growing up, but he's sure made certain he's an active part of our lives now."

"He and Ruth are wonderful."

"And Dev," Abby said.

Caroline and Michelle laughed and exchanged glances. "Yes, Dev's wonderful--and you better keep thinking that."

"I will. All my life," she vowed.

When the knock came on the door, Penny opened it and reached up her arms. Samuel and Ruth had instantly taken to the little girl, declaring they were pleased as punch to have a ready-made granddaughter. The first of many, they hoped. Samuel leaned over to pick her up, and smiled at the picture his three daughters made.

"I wish your mother could see you three today. You're all so beautiful. She'd have been proud of what you've done with your lives."

"Thanks, Dad." Caroline crossed the room and reached up to kiss his cheek. "I don't want to rush anything, but is it time to start?"

"Can't wait for me to tie the knot?" Abby teased as she followed, kissing Sam on his other cheek.

"Remember how Caroline has always mothered us?" Michelle asked, following suit, then relieving him of Penny. "I think she just wants to know you're safely on your way."

Abby nodded. "I'm very ready. Can you believe we pulled this off in under three months?"

Michelle set Penny on her feet, handing her the basket of flower petals. "I believe it. I've spent every free moment on the phone following up on things."

The sound of the church organ could be heard as Caroline followed behind Michelle. "All happiness, sis."

Abby linked arms with her father, smiling up at him.

"This makes the day perfect. Thank you for walking me down the aisle," she said softly.

"It hasn't come any time too soon, you know," he said softly as they moved into place at the end of the aisle. "Dev has about driven us crazy with missing you. At least things can settle down once you two are married and living together in Houston. And I'll have one of my babies close at hand."

The music swelled as they started down the aisle. Abby smiled at her friends gathered on either side, and then let her gaze rest on Dev. Her heart skipped a beat, then began to race. Her hands grew damp, and her breathing became difficult. He was as gorgeous as the first time she saw him. And her heart almost burst with happiness and love. She knew over the recent months things had been settled between them. Her love grew each day. She trusted his did as well. Now their life together began.

Dev watched, giving nothing away with his expression as her father escorted her down the aisle. Ruth sat in the front row of the groom's side. Samuel was planning to sit with Brandon and Josh on the front row of the bride's side.

But Abby didn't care about any of it now. She had eyes only for Dev. When her father handed her to him, her happiness was complete.

"Dearly beloved," began the minister.

Dev leaned close. "That's you, Abby, you are my dearly beloved."

With those words, she knew he'd finally, fully forgiven her deception. Life was wonderful.

Epilogue

The nurse behind the counter looked up, widening her eyes at the sight of an entire wedding party descending on her.

"We're here to see Caroline Madison," Michelle said.

"And baby," Josh added.

"We were told visiting hours started at seven."

"Yes," said the nurse, the puzzlement obvious in her eyes. "She and the baby are in room 234. Usually we limit the number of visitors--"

"She'll want to see us, we're all her family."

"And I'm the baby's cousin," Penny said from her perch in her father's arms.

"We'd have come right away when she was admitted, but we had the reception to see to," Ruth explained. "We couldn't dash out and leave all the guests."

"She was already in the beginning stages of labor during the ceremony, but didn't want to take the limelight away from us," Abby said. "She was my matron of honor."

"Oh, well, go right down the hall, it's the fourth door on the left," the nurse said, obviously not clear on the situation despite the hurried explanations.

Everyone crowded into Caroline's room. Abby and Dev hugged her, then Michelle and Josh and Penny. When Samuel drew her into his arms, she began to cry. Brandon held her hand and handed her a handkerchief. Ruth gave her a quick kiss.

"I want to see my grandson," Samuel said, peering into the bassinet beside the bed.

Brandon lifted the tiny infant, holding him with confidence. "John Samuel Madison, meet your grandfather."

Samuel's eyes grew suspiciously moist as he gazed around the gathering of his family.

"I never expected this day. I am truly blessed."

Caroline, Michelle and Abby smiled. "Welcome to the family, Dad," they said in unison.

—The End—

More books by Barbara McMahon

Bayou Nights
Letters to Caroline
Michelle's Marriage Deal
Trusting Abby

The Harts of Texas Series
Rebel Heart
Tangled Hearts
Reckless Heart

Cowboy Heroes Series
Blue Bells on the Hill
Cowboy's Bride
One Stubborn Cowboy
Crazy About a Cowboy
Never Doubt a Cowboy
Cowboy Marshal
Summer Cowboy
Second Chance Cowboy
Movie Star Cowboy

Tropical Escape Series
Island Rendezvous
Come into the Sun
Island Paradise
Destination Romance Boxed Set